Almost

Also by Montana Carr

Beyond the Scent of Sugar: A Memoir by Billie River

Marti Starova Erotic Thrillers

Drowning in Broad Daylight (Book 1)

Shadow Work (Book 2)

Rain-Soaked (Book 3)

Coming Soon!

The Familiar Dark (Book 5) - March 11, 2026

Almost

A Marti Starova Erotic Thriller Book 4

Montana Carr

Northshore Noir Press

Northshore Noir Press
Toronto, Canada
www.northshorenoir.com

ISBN: 978-1-998648-25-2

eBook ISBN: 978-1-998648-26-9

For more information visit: northshorenoir.com

Contents

Chapter 1

"Why the fuck is there shit in my office?" Marti shouted. She stood with a cigarette in one hand and a coffee in the other, staring.

"Oh sorry, that's mine," Lori said from the other room. The words were casual, causing Marti to blink in bewilderment.

Marti looked again at the plastic box with a log of excrement. She wrinkled her nose at the unpleasant stench that faintly tainted the otherwise familiar scent of cigarettes and drugs. Scrunching her face up in distaste, she swiveled on her heels and retraced her steps back through the door that separated the two offices. "Why the fuck did you shit in my office?"

"That's not what I meant," Lori said, without looking up from her computer. "It's not mine. It's Bertha's."

"Bertha crapped in my office?"

"Yes, and it took me a while to convince her. Let me tell you."

Marti Starova looked at the clock and then back at Lori. "It's been almost twenty-three hours since I've had a hit of Shadow," she said. She'd been trying for a couple of weeks to cut back on the drug, and this was the longest sober stretch she'd had in years. She struggled to make sense of what Lori was saying.

Lori Harring was her reliable, predictable secretary. They had been through so much together recently, Marti was developing feelings for her, and vice versa. And Marti hated feelings. "Is this what conversation is like when people are sober? Because fuck that."

"What?" Lori asked, finally looking up from her keyboard. "I don't understand."

"You don't understand? Well, I don't fucking understand! Why is there a box of shit in my office?"

Lori laughed and got up from her desk. "I told you, Bertha. Bertha Tinkledorp. Bertha?" Lori repeated, as if saying the word again would tweak a memory. "The cat I've been trying to rescue."

With deliberate nonchalance, Marti took a hard drag of her cigarette and blew the smoke into Lori's face. Years ago, tobacco manufacturers changed the chemical formula for cigarettes. Second-hand smoke was now harmless. But a face full of smoke could still send a message. Lori huffed and waved at the air.

"Get that shit out of my office," Marti said.

Lori headed into Marti's office and looked out the open window. Marti followed, if only to stare at Lori's ass. "I'm trying to get Bertha to come in, to rescue her. So I am giving her a litter box."

"That cat hates you," Marti said as she sat on the couch. She spilled a bit of coffee on her jeans, and then spilled more on the floor when she wiped at her jeans.

"But she likes you, and this is your office. I thought she might like to come in out of the rain," Lori explained. She leaned further out the window hopes to spying the cat.

Marti leaned forward. Her lips parted as Lori bent further out the window. She could almost feel the supple skin of Lori's thigh, and she licked her lips in anticipation before shaking her head to clear the vision. "Why aren't you offering food? Wouldn't that tempt the cat more?"

"Cat food stinks," Lori said.

"And shit doesn't? Lori Harring, do you have a kink I don't know about?" Marti teased.

Lori drew her head back inside the office. "If I say yes, would you finally go out on a date with me?"

"No. Why are you asking me? Why have you started asking me out on dates?" Marti was very matter-of-fact. She refused all of Lori's advances. Marti had already lost two secretaries to her own lust and toxic behavior. She did not want to lose this one.

"My therapist said I should–"

"Therapist?"

"Yes, therapist. She said understanding oneself, including attributes and inclinations, guides the choice of joys to pursue. Confidence in one's competence shapes how individuals approach joys, work towards progress, and respond to challenges related to those joys," Lori said.

"Inclinations?" Marti asked.

"Within the paradigm of humanistic psychology, which places a central emphasis on the realization of one's inherent potential and personal development, the acknowledgment and acceptance of individual inclinations are posited as pivotal mechanisms that engender authenticity," Lori said.

"Riiiight," Marti replied. She had tuned out as soon as Lori started talking about paradigms and not sexual inclinations. "Get the box of crap out of my office, now."

Lori reluctantly grabbed the litter box and moved it into her own office. "Not good enough," Marti said. She took another drag and shook her finger. "No cat shit anywhere in Martina Starova Investigations."

Lori cautiously carried the green plastic box of sand and feces out of the office. "Fine, but don't blame me if the cat gets hit by a car or something," she said over her shoulder on the way out to the garbage dumpster.

Marti turned back to her work. The paper coffee cup sat cooling on Marti's desk, her coffee's bitterness a counterpoint to the treacle taste of her current case. Marcel Dupont owned the esteemed "L'Étoile d'Argent" restaurant. He'd sought her help to combat a slew of malicious reviews that had marred his establishment's reputation. The accusations ranged from dubious ingredient choices to unfounded criminal connections.

Marti's focused gaze scoured the reviews on her screen. One authored by the anonymous "GourmetCritique55," struck her as potentially defamatory.

"Last week, I hit up this place called L'Étoile d'Argent. Belmont Heights spent centuries building their reputation, and this place torched it in one disgusting appetizer. Seriously though, you wouldn't even believe it–they're whipping out bread with a green mold creeping on it. No joke, it's a total horror show; the stuff of nightmares in broad daylight! Right after eating there, my stomach went on its own rebellion: think of a critical case of food poisoning. If dumpster fire had an address, then L'Étoile d'Argent would be ground zero—a disaster zone where good dining goes to die."

It sounded like a damned teenager and completely unimportant. With a shrug, Marti saved the review into a folder. Boring. But it paid the bills.

The monotony of sifting through GourmetCritique55's endless reviews about L'Étoile d'Argent gnawed at Marti's patience. She combed through the digital maze, bored and indifferent. The allure of Shadow whispered to her, promising a temporary escape from the tedium. "I can't do this," she said as she got out of her chair.

"Lori, I'm heading to that restaurant. I'm going to expense it, since, you know, work," Marti said with a laugh. "I'll call you on my way over. You figure out what I should eat."

On the drive over, Marti had Lori advise her what kind of food to order. "Don't order booze. You have to drive. Plus, it's expensive," Lori cautioned. "You want watercress soup, a quiche, and a salad. They'll provide bread."

"Thanks." Marti took a last drag off her cigarette and dropped it into a coffee cup that served as a car ashtray. Parking in the restaurant's lot, she got out of the car.

Marti opened the trunk and rifled through a duffel bag of clothes. She found a bright purple shirt–wrinkle-free, of course–and, with a quick look around, doffed her t-shirt and put on the fresh shirt. Leaving her t-shirt and jacket in the trunk, she headed into L'Étoile d'Argent.

Marti walked up to the hostess desk and smiled. "For one," she said.

The woman smiled back and pushed her glasses up her nose. "One. This way, please," she said, gathering a menu and leading Marti through the tables. There were only a few empty tables. "Is this okay?" the hostess asked.

"Yes, thanks."

"Any time," she said as she put the menu on the table. She put her hand on Marti's shoulder as she walked past. Marti scanned the menu as she waited for the server. He wasn't long in coming.

"Hello, my name is Hamilton. Welcome to L'Étoile d'Argent, your afternoon star. Can I get you something to start?" Hamilton raised an inquisitive brow. A habit he picked up from years in the theater before becoming a server here.

"A coffee," Marti answered, her eyes darting to the menu. She paused as the silence inflated between them.

Hamilton's eyes roamed over Marti, taking in her looks, before he averted his gaze to the menu she was holding.

"We have a special blend that I think you'll love," Hamilton suggested, his voice smooth and alluring.

Marti nodded, not even bothering to look up from the menu. As he walked away to prepare her coffee, she looked for the menu items Lori had recommended.

When Hamilton returned with her coffee, he leaned a little too close, brushing her arm. "Is there anything else I can get for you?" he asked, his voice low and seductive.

Marti felt a shiver of revulsion run down her spine. "What?"

Hamilton smirked, believing in his unabashed sexiness. "If you want me, just whistle," he said before walking away, leaving Marti to contemplate the dangerous thoughts swirling in her mind. Thoughts like If I had my gun I'd probably shoot him, and I think I will whistle for that asshole.

Marti stuck her fingers in her mouth, pressed against her tongue, and let out an ear-piercing whistle.

"I'll have the watercress soup, quiche, and French leaf salad please, Hamilton," she said when he arrived. "And a whiskey. Please."

With that, he was gone, leaving Marti with nothing but the echo of her orders. Her choice bewildered her; she had no idea what watercress tasted like and her experience with quiche was limited to bleary Sunday morning cooking shows. As for French leaf salad, well…

Her mind lost in thought, Marti watched as customers moved smoothly among the tables, mouthing 'Hello' to others and giving small waves. They navigated this world effortlessly while she felt like an alien.

Except for Henry fucking Gardner. What was that piece of shit doing here? Marti glared at him from across the restaurant, though he remained oblivious to her. Henry and…who the fuck was he with? Marti didn't recognize any of them, other than general thug faces. Broken nose here, cauliflower ear there.

She'd been hired to find Henry after he disappeared. Daddy Kevin wasn't happy that Henry kidnapped and assaulted Marti. He was even less happy to find out Henry was selling his drug recipes to the competition.

Gotta love family loyalty. At least Kevin hadn't killed his son. Yet.

Chapter 2

Marti was almost enjoying the ambience of the restaurant as she waited for her meal. Whoever the online critic was, Marti figured they had never actually been inside.

"Martina?"

Marti looked up. "Mary! Cliff! How are you?" she said as she rose from her chair.

"Martina, I almost didn't recognize you without that jacket of yours. How are you?" Mary gushed as she wrapped her arms around Marti. Marti hugged her back. "Oh, my gosh. It's been what? Almost a year?"

"It sure has been a while. It's lovely to see you." Marti stepped back and put her hand out to shake Cliff's hand.

Marti met Cliff and Mary Kogoya after Charlie Gomes had escaped police custody. She met them after he killed their young daughter, Sabrina. After he ripped the little girl's heart out. After they'd arrested him.

She met the parents when she went to their home with Detective Damien Kane. She met Mary when she wailed upon hearing about her daughter. She met Cliff when he shook and collapsed and puked on her shoes.

"Would you like to join me?" Marti said, gesturing to her table.

"We've just finished, but thank you," Mary said, still hanging onto Marti's arm. Marti was used to it. Some relatives of homicide victims, especially parents, liked to hang onto her as if doing so would let them hang onto their loved ones a little longer.

"I have to check the car. Parking tickets, you know," Cliff said as he headed out.

Mary waved a dismissive hand. "You know him. Listen, are we going to see you later, on Sabrina's anniversary?"

"Of course," Marti said. She visited the Kogoyas every year on the anniversary of Sabrina's death, even though she left the force in disgrace.

Marti wanted to tell them everything. She wanted to tell them it was Damian Kane who let Gomes escape. Kane who let him kill their daughter. Not Marti. Marti was not responsible. She was set up. She cleared her name.

But she knew they didn't give a fuck. They still talked to her. They did not blame her.

Mary gave her a peck on the cheek. "Excellent. I have to run. See you soon." Mary headed out while Marti returned to her food.

Hamilton appeared with a smile. "Your soup," he said, placing a bowl in front of Marti. There was a note tucked beneath it.

"Interested in dessert? Hostess Barbara."

Marti looked up, spotted Barbara watching her, and raised the note slightly. Barbara smiled, too broadly.

Barbara made her way over, glancing around like she was sneaking contraband. Marti followed her gaze, not sure why dessert needed stealth.

"I've got twenty minutes. I'm off the clock," Barbara said.

"Twenty minutes," Marti repeated, still unsure what was happening.

"This way," Barbara said, nodding. She led Marti past the hostess desk. Hamilton winked. She headed into a narrow hallway. They ducked into a multi-use washroom. Barbara shut the door behind them.

Barbara cupped Marti's face. "Those lips are amazing," she murmured, then kissed her. Hard, then soft, then deliberately. She bit Marti's lower lip gently and let it go.

Marti kissed her back, parting her lips. Barbara sucked her tongue deep, urgent now, exploring her mouth.

"Fuck. Don't stop kissing me."

Marti brushed her lips over Barbara's, teasing, pulling away, then letting her bite. Her skin felt like Shadow slipping down her throat. Marti ran her hands down Barbara's curves, fingertips finding stiff nipples under the thin shirt. Barbara gasped, breath catching as Marti's lips found skin.

Barbara gripped Marti's face tighter, hips shifting. Marti sealed her mouth over hers, swallowed her moan. Her breath was hot in Marti's ear.

Marti looked quickly at the door. Force of habit.

"Touch me," Barbara whispered, still clinging to Marti's cheeks.

She pulled Marti's hand down, guiding it inside her pants. Her back arched slightly. Marti's fingers found the edge of panties and the coarse hair beneath. She tugged gently as their mouths locked again.

But the angles were wrong, Barbara still wouldn't let go of her face, and Marti gave up the attempt. This was going to stay a fucking make-out session. Fine. She leaned into it.

"Kiss me," Barbara said again.

Marti gripped her hips, kissed her like she was working clit with tongue. Deep, slow, deliberate. She slid her hands up under Barbara's shirt and into her bra, thumbing her nipples as she kissed harder, rougher.

Their tongues fucked, fought, surrendered. Barbara's body rocked with the rhythm. Her moans grew louder, breath hitching. Finally, with a trembling push, she broke the kiss.

Marti leaned back, lips slick. Barbara's hand hovered near her own mouth.

"Wish I could cut these off and take the, with me," Barbara whispered, tracing Marti's lips.

What the fuck?

Marti smiled. "They're taken, for now. Maybe next time I'm here?"

"Absolutely."

Marti took a quick look in the mirror, splashed some water on her face, and adjusted her shirt. With a wink, she walked out, heading through the restaurant. She paid Hamilton quickly for the meal she didn't eat and left. As soon as she was outside, she lit a cigarette and got into her car.

"...the body of suspected drug kingpin Trevor Dunnigan, believed to be behind the spread of Fentafill and MethLumina in Falls City, was discovered early this morning—"

Marti slapped the radio off. "I don't give a fuck," she muttered, jamming the key in the ignition. She drove away without looking back.

Chapter 3

The makeout session at the restaurant's bathroom was something Marti wouldn't try again. Barbara was attractive, but the whole thing seemed too set up. It might have been recorded, Marti thought. Turning away from the office window, Marti inhaled deeply from her cigarette. Marti looked at her desk drawer. It was an irresistible abyss, where every hit promised escape. She reached in and took out her inhaler.

As Marti inhaled the potent fumes of Shadow, an eerie calm settled over her. The world took on a surreal, dark-hued beauty, where her senses blurred. Time warped, and the weight of her burdens momentarily lifted in a seductive dance of illusion.

In this altered state, she floated through a dreamscape of shifting shadows. The boundaries between reality and imagination became indistinguishable. Her troubles seemed to dissolve into the mist that enveloped her consciousness. It left behind a haunting sense of detachment and an insatiable craving for the ephemeral escape.

A knock at her office door startled Marti into reality. Lori opened the door. "Are you able to meet with the new client?" she asked.

"Do they have an appointment?" Marti asked.

Lori stepped in and leaned towards Marti. "Yes, Henrick Katsaros, ten minutes ago. You good?"

Marti nodded. "Out in two minutes. I have to pee," she said, retreating to the bathroom. Marti loved Shadow because it was so much like a long-winded orgasm: pleasurable, but you could pull yourself out of it if you needed to. Though sometimes it didn't work and it wasn't even edging. Marti composed herself, splashed cold water on her face, and walked into Lori's office.

"Mr. Katsaros, nice to meet you. I'm Martina Starova."

"Nice to meet you. Please, call me Henrick." Henrick's unassuming gaze met Marti's with a hesitant nod as he awkwardly extended his hand. Marti extended her hand to grasp his and almost recoiled as she touched his sweaty palm.

"Thanks Henrick. Call me Marti. How can I help you today?" she asked as she sat in a chair.

"I'd like to know that my parents are okay," Henrick began. "Andreas and Isabella Katsaros. They came to Falls City for two weeks of vacation and haven't been in touch. We're from Upper Henley. It's very unusual for my mother not to call. They travel frequently. Well, my father does, but any time my mother goes with him, she calls. She calls or messages me twice a day. Once at noon and once at midnight. I last heard from her two days ago," he said as he glanced at his phone.

Henrick rearranged himself in his chair and watched Marti's every move. Upper Henley was a tony suburb for people who played at being rich but couldn't quite afford the real thing.

Marti pulled a crinkled pack of cigarettes from a pocket and her fingers fished through for a single smoke. She lit the cigarette and blew smoke through her nose. Marti looked first at the toe of her boot, then at the table in front of her. And waited.

"You are quite...different, aren't you?" Henrick asked.

"I'm doing you a huge favor. No one knows Falls City like I do. When you want to find someone in a sea of five million someones, you need a different someone like me to find them."

Henrick wrinkled his nose in disgust as Marti blew more smoke. "I just want to know they're okay."

"Yes, you said that. Can I see the last message your mother sent?" Marti asked.

"Yes, of course," Henrick said, pulling up the message and handing over his phone. "I know two days isn't much, but this is Falls City. Anything could have gone wrong. No offense intended."

"None taken," Marti said as she handed the phone to Lori. Lori took a photograph of the simple text Henrick had received.

"Hi Henrick, just checking in again. Hope you're doing well. Falls City is quite something. I'm enjoying the sights. Love, Mom."

Henrick's brows furrowed with worry as he spoke. "My mother hasn't sent any more messages, and I'm getting concerned. I've called the Neiman-Costi hotel, but they claim they have no guests by the name of Katsaros." Henrick double-checked his phone, as if it might have an answer for him this time.

Marti, perched in the worn leather armchair, took a drag from her cigarette, exhaling a cloud of smoke that blended with the muted ambiance. "Hotels value privacy. They would never tell a stranger that any particular person was there." Marti absent-mindedly flicked ashes onto the floor.

Lori leaned forward and handed Henrick his phone. She gave Marti a dirty look for putting ashes on the floor. "Have your parents ever traveled under aliases?" she inquired.

Henrick rubbed his forehead, confusion and worry playing across his face. "No, not that I know of. We're well-off, so it could be something terrible. I can't help but think of the worst-case scenarios—kidnapping or mugging."

"And you've been to the police?"

"Yes, of course. After the hotel said they weren't there, I called the Missing Persons department. But they said that two adults can get away for a while and refused to take a report," Henrick said. He turned and looked at Marti. "Why wouldn't they even take a report?"

Marti offered a sympathetic smile as she flicked the ash from her cigarette into a nearby ashtray this time. With a calm demeanor, she commented she had seen this before. "The police can be indifferent in cases like this. They often need more than just concern to take action. I'll take the case for $50,000."

"Fifty thousand? No. I don't like your terms," Henrick said. His hand flung out dismissively against the cheap side table that wobbled under the weight of his discontent. The dim neon haze outside the window flickered with uncertainty, casting an eerie glow. His worried face now seethed with frustration and disbelief. "I'm not asking you to kill them."

"The only people who don't like my terms are the ones with lots of money. It's like a personal affront to expect them to part with it. So let me change the terms for you. It's $50,000 to locate your parents and give you proof they are alive. And every time you question my fee, it goes up by a thousand," Marti said.

Henrick stood up and headed to the door. When his hand got to the knob, Marti added, "Off to get more police help, then?" An ash fell onto her jeans and she brushed it onto the floor. Henrick paused, turned, and returned to the chair.

"Fifty thousand. Have you heard of GenoHealth Solutions?"

"No," Marti said, stubbing her cigarette out.

"My father, Andreas, is the CEO and owner of GenoHealth Solutions. They are a major genomics company in the New Dutch City. They produce personalized medical treatments based on genetics. For very wealthy clients, of course. After standard health care costs were mandated by the government, the real money ended up being in customized treatments. It's worth about three billion dollars. Both he and my mother came to Falls City for a vacation.

And before you ask, no, the company won't handle this. This happened on personal time, so they said it's up to me. Choosing to vacation in this city was a terrible choice. I need them found without fuss."

Wrinkling her brow, Marti glanced down at the state of her chipped nail. She'd have to file it smooth before she could use it properly. "Hold up. Did you legit go to the cops?" she asked.

Henrick traced idle circles on the weathered leather armrest of his chair, fingertips vibrating slightly against the worn surface. Air blew from his parted lips in a throaty whistle as he replied, "Yes." She knew he was lying.

"It won't help if you lie to us," Lori said. "It can only set us back. Before we go any further, you'll have to pay the fee. Cash, not credit. The account is R4ND-7O9M5N3A8N." Lori's annoyance amused Marti.

"R4ND? A cryptocurrency account. Yes, fine, I can do that," Henrick said. Marti was glad he knew what it was, as it revealed more about his character. While he fiddled with paying, Marti retreated to her office and poured herself a whiskey. An afternoon shot always lightened her day. The first sip came as a bolt–fiery warmth spread across her tongue before sinking into her belly, painting lazy strokes of comfort on its way down. It tasted of robust oak-aged honesty, interwoven with subtle hints of spice-laced mystery. She walked back to Lori and Henrick.

Lori nodded to Marti. She had received the payment. "Okay Henrick, I'll need photos, credit card statements for the last week, an itinerary if they had one," Lori said.

"Copies of texts since they left, too. How were they before they left? Did everything seem normal?" Marti asked.

"Yes, completely normal," he replied. "They've been gone four days."

Marti said, "You were smart to get in touch with us. They've been gone for four days, two of which were spent without contact. And they still have another ten before they come back home. Hopefully, they're okay."

"We'll need to get some basic info from you as well. Height, weight, age. Friends, family contacts. I have a form for you to complete," Lori said as she clicked away at the computer.

"Take this phone," she said, pulling a disposable phone from her desk drawer. "It's programmed with our number for you to call if anything happens. Keep it on you all the time and don't use it for any other calls. Don't answer any other calls. Only if it shows Starova on the display. No one can track your movements because I've disabled tracking. At the end of the case, take out the card like this," she said, popping the small card out. "Snap it in half and throw everything away," she continued as she put the card back in and turned the phone on.

"Why the trickery with phones?" Henrick asked as he pocketed the device.

"You said no one in the company would help. That they won't help find the company owner is very concerning," Marti said. "This way, your information, and privacy, are under your control."

"How long do you think it will take?"

"There's no telling. I'll keep you updated."

"Daily?"

"Yes if you'd like. Lori will call you every day to give you an update. You will get an invoice if there are any extraordinary expenses," Marti said.

"What's extraordinary?"

"If my car gets shot up by the baddies, and my insurance won't cover it, then it's yours. That would be extraordinary."

"Could that happen?"

"It could, but it won't."

"Alright, thank you," Henrick said, and walked out the door.

"So what do you think?" Lori asked once he was gone.

"I think there is way more than meets the eye. Way more. The head of a three billion dollar company neither of us has heard of, gone. And the company won't help? Create a file, send me an initial report." She got up and headed to her office.

Chapter 4

While she waited for Lori's report, Marti began organizing and writing out the restaurant report. All that was left was to identify the online troll.

"Have you thought any more about my offer?" Lori called from her office.

"Which offer are you talking about this time?" Marti asked.

"A date. To go out on an actual date with me."

"The last time we went for coffee, we both got shot," Marti said.

"Yeah. That wasn't exactly the kind of heart pounding experience I was hoping for," Lori responded.

Marti laughed, got up, and shut her door without further comment. It signified to Lori that Marti wanted 'alone' time, which usually meant drugs. But not this time. Marti took another sip of whiskey and lit a cigarette.

That woman.

Marti sat on the couch, unzipped her jeans, and pictured Lori performing a striptease for her.

Marti closed her eyes and saw Lori the way she liked to: lean, slow-moving, hips swaying to a rhythm only Marti knew. Shirt unbuttoned one-handed, bra dangling, tits round and freckled like she wanted. Smoke on her breath, whiskey on her lips. Marti imagined tasting both.

Lori peeled off her underwear with the deliberateness. Slow, confident, no need to perform. Just heat, thick and real.

Marti slipped a hand past the waistband of her jeans, fingers quick and practiced. She wasn't thinking about love. Just skin. Just friction. She moved in time with the image. Lori climbing onto her lap, knees on either side, eyes locked.

She imagined Lori's mouth at her throat, her breath warm and damp. The kind of touch that left bruises in the shape of want. Marti pressed harder. No sweetness. No sighs. Just the sound of her own breath getting ragged. Just the pressure building and snapping like a blown fuse.

After, she lay still for a beat, her hand sticky and useless, Lori already fading like smoke in the dark.

Thirty minutes later, Lori knocked on the door and walked in without an invitation. Marti noticed the slightly disappointed look on her face upon finding Marti at her computer. "The files are ready."

"Good, sit. Let's go over the next steps," Marti said. "What do we have?"

"GenoHealth is a very controversial company. They offer customized medicine and face constant criticism for their high prices. Lots of stories about single moms with dying kids pleading for help," Lori said.

"Such philanthropists. And the credit statements?"

"Four days ago, there's a credit card charge at the Windmill Hotel on Forty-eighth. Very average hotel, nothing special. Not what you'd expect from billionaires."

"Henrick said he called Neiman-Costi, and the charge is for Windmill. Got it. Go on," Marti said. "What was the amount for the Windmill?"

"Five hundred. Enough for two nights."

"So they were only planning to be there for two days. What's on the credit statements after that?" Marti asked.

"Nothing. They fall off the radar," Lori said. "No purchases, no cash withdrawals, no texts."

"Nothing at all? Not food, not travel, nothing? That's not good. Anything else?"

"Andreas had some kind of trouble ten years ago, but it seems corporate. There were reports of a copyright issue in business newspapers, but they settled it out of court. He's been clean since," Lori said.

"Send me some photos. Try to find out more about the copyright issue. And get the names of the aggrieved single moms from this year. I'll head to the Windmill," Marti said.

"Did you think any more about that offer?" Lori asked as she got up to leave.

"I did, thanks," Marti said as she licked her fingers.

Marti left the office and drove to the Windmill Hotel. She didn't know the place, which made it unlikely she'd get any information from the staff. Once parked, she studied the photos of Andreas and Isabella Katsaros.

Andreas was fifty-one, had neat, salt-and-pepper hair and a weak jawline. Brown eyes, the left one drooping down a little. He had an olive complexion and a little too much red around the nose to not have a drug problem. Like his eye, his left ear was off. He was slender and on the short side for a man. Maybe Marti's height, based on the car in the background of the photo.

Isabella was forty-nine. There was not a trace of gray in her long chestnut hair. She had brown eyes, laugh lines, and thick lips. As Marti moved the photo around, she zoomed in and saw a café au lait birthmark on her neck.

A light fog rolled in, and Marti shivered. She left her jacket in the trunk of her car to look less like a visitor, and wore a tight button-up shirt. Marti lit a cigarette and timed her entrance to arrive just before a family walked in. She held the door for them and walked in after them.

Marti looked quickly for the hotel bar and made a bee-line. Typical hotel bar patrons. The drunken men in suits were loud and friendly while the barfly at the end of the bar was sullen. The suit guys might be more willing to talk. She undid a button on her shirt, zhuzhed her hair, and walked over.

"Hey boys, can you help me find my friends?" Marti asked. She smiled and waited while they took her in. She wasn't at her best, but good enough for beer goggles.

"Yeah, yeah, sit down. How can we help you, darling?"

Marti sat down on his lap, eliciting hoots and cheers. She pulled out her phone and showed him the photo. He put his hands around her waist and leaned in to see. "No, I can't say I have," he said. "Guys? Anyone know her friends?"

Marti handed her phone off but kept an eye on it while it made the rounds.

"Hey yes! They left yesterday. I remember because I helped carry her bags. Her husband wouldn't help her. He was a dick," one man said.

"Lots of bags?" Marti asked as she squirmed off her companion's lap. She winked and whispered, "Thanks for the ride, but you might want to wait a bit before you stand up."

"Just three bags, but heavy. A lady like that shouldn't be hauling around heavy stuff," he said as he handed Marti her phone. "Are you staying?" he asked.

"Sorry, no, I have to find my friends. Thanks. Did they drive their own car?"

"Taxi. Blue & White."

"Gentlemen, it's been a thrill," she said as she headed out.

Marti called her contact at Blue & White. She had been diligent about keeping in touch with the contacts she had made as a homicide detective. She had lost touch when she lost her job, but then found them all again. Marti needed them even more now she was a private investigator. As a citizen, it cost her more money to get information, but it was of a much better quality than she ever got as a cop.

"Rudy? It's Marti Starova. I need to know about a trip. It's worth a hundred," she said after reaching him on the phone. Marti sat in her car smoking while Rudy went through his database of calls. There were three pickups from the Windmill right around check out time. She took all the details and sent Rudy his money.

Paying off informants was so much easier now than when she was a cop.

She texted Lori the addresses and waited. In just a few minutes, Lori called.

"The address on Chilov Street is a restaurant, the Prawn. The address is on Link Street. It's a boutique hotel, The Sophet. And the last one, on Render Road, is an art gallery," Lori said.

"Right, The Sophet seems the most likely destination. I'll head over there and do an old-fashioned stake out," Marti said.

"In the meantime, I'll try to figure out why there are no taxi charges, hotel, restaurant, or art gallery charges on their cards, and no large cash withdrawal at the start of adventure time," Lori said.

Night settled in and the headlights of cars on the streets ricocheted off puddles and windows, creating an ever-moving kaleidoscope. After twenty minutes, Marti drove past the 'Welcome to Baldwin Vista Neighborhood' sign. She knew they didn't mean it. Marti pulled onto Link Street.

The traffic was as heavy here as on any of Falls City's main roads. Most of the cars were taxis and limousine services. They stopped, dropped off their clients, and drove away. Everyone walked to a large, unremarkable building near The Sophet. They were greeted at the door and vanished inside. There was nowhere for Marti to park her car, making the surveillance harder.

Marti finally found a parking spot three blocks away. She took a hit of Shadow and headed back to Link Street with a small camera. Marti found a dark doorway near The Sophet and settled in for a long wait. It was going to be boring. This was a shit batch of Shadow. No effect at all.

Chapter 5

Marti waited in the drizzling rain while on the stakeout. She hated the boring work more because she knew she couldn't risk getting too high, and she especially hated having to wait in the elements. It was three hours before Andreas and Isabella walked out of The Sophet. Delighted, Marti got to her feet, ready to creep along the walls in pursuit.

The short distance they walked down the street surprised and disappointed her. It was not quite what she expected. Marti squinted in confusion as they joined a long line before disappearing inside the same nondescript building many others had. They had displayed a pass, an invitation or maybe a ticket, before slipping into anonymity amongst countless others. The question rolled around Marti's mind like tumbleweed in a desert land-scape: What the hell was going on inside there?

While brooding over this peculiarity, she pulled out a cigarette, igniting it with the deftness only years of habit can teach you. She crept away from the mystery building, cloaking herself in an aloofness intended to blend with oblivious bystanders. She heard footsteps coming up be-hind her. Two people, synchronized steps but different footwear.

"Is this her?"

Marti whirled around, ready to punch. She saw Athena first, then another woman, smaller, rougher. "You're the bitch that fucked my wife?" she asked.

Marti's eyes shot to Athena, who gave only a slight smile. Marti wasn't sure if she should answer the ques-tion because she wasn't sure which answer might get her punched. She finally decided. "If she's pregnant, the baby isn't mine."

"Ha! You're right Athena, I do like her. My name's Muriel. Call me Mure," she said, holding out her hand. Marti was relieved and shook hands. Mure was wearing a black silk dress with a rising side slit. The plunging neck-line revealed a bustier. She had a thin leather and ruby collar tight around her neck. Her black, shoulder length hair was thick and natural. She was a stunner.

"Marti. Nice to meet you," she said.

Athena stepped up and kissed Marti. "What brings you to this neighborhood?" she asked.

"I want in there," Marti said, pointing with her head toward the building.

Mure laughed. "Goddam Athena, you really can pick them." She grabbed Marti by the waist and ran her hands along Marti's back. "Skinny, though."

Athena walked behind Marti and pressed in, running her hand along Marti's stomach. "That just makes her easier to maul," she said, biting her ear. "You up to a threesome? We can bring you inside."

"Fuck yeah," Marti said. "What's inside?"

"Sex."

"Awesome. My rules are, just the two of you; no torture; if I say no, I mean it; and never bind both my hands at once."

With Mure on one side and Athena on the other, Marti strode toward the nondescript brick building tucked away between two warehouses. There were no signs, just a single black-glass door with a brass plaque that read "Invitation Only." It felt more like a private banker's office than anything erotic.

She was grateful the women invited her; places like this weren't ones you stumbled into. They were whispered about. Athena flashed her invite from a sleek black card-holder and nodded toward Marti.

"This is our plus-one," she said smoothly, sliding the card into a reader beside the door.

The doorman's eyes flicked to his screen, nodded and smiled. "Standard rules apply. Enthusiastic consent only, respect all boundaries. No names. If you recognize someone, no you don't." He pressed a button under his desk, unlocking the inner doorway with a soft click.

Inside, the building pulsed with pleasure. Ecstatic moans drifted down the corridor like incense, mixing with low music and laughter. Every door was closed, but the hallway itself seemed to breathe with restrained decadence.

Inside, the building pulsed with pleasure. Ecstatic moans drifted down the corridor like incense, mixing with low music and laughter. Every door was closed, but nothing was soundproofed. Not really. The hallway itself seemed to breathe with restrained decadence.

Marti's stomach flipped, caught somewhere between nerves and fascination. It wasn't her first time in a sex club, but this place felt different. More hidden, more... curated.

"Check-in is up here," Athena said over her shoulder, gesturing toward a small alcove just off the main corridor. The reception area was minimal but lush: mahogany paneling, leather benches, and a wall of gleaming metal lockers, each one fingerprint-activated and unnumbered for privacy. A nod to luxury disguised as anonymity.

"Phones, IDs, any electronics, go in here," the attendant said without looking up from his tablet. "No cameras. No scanning devices. No questions."

"Security theater," Mure muttered under her breath with a grin. "What matters here is discretion."

Marti placed her phone in one locker along with her Shadow inhaler, cigarettes, and quietly slid in her gun too. She hesitated for just a second before pressing her finger to seal it up. If Athena or Mure noticed what she brought in, they didn't comment.

As they moved away from reception, Marti asked quietly, "How long has this place been running? Why haven't I heard about it?"

"Six months," Mure replied. "It's not advertised anywhere. You need an invite from someone who's already trusted inside. And once you're in, you can buy your next entry... assuming you play nice."

Athena added as she adjusted her bag: "Everyone can watch anything as close as they want, but you don't touch unless you get consent first."

"That sounds simple," Marti said softly.

Athena gave an amused hum that somehow sounded both approving and skeptical at once.

Moments later she returned from speaking briefly with another staffer and held up a smooth plastic keycard that caught the hallway lighting like glassy ice.

"This way." She shifted her heavy rubber duffel higher onto her shoulder, a gesture that made something metallic thud faintly within it, and led them down another hallway lined with dim reddish lights above each doorframe.

"You better be worth the cost of the upgrade," Athena said over her shoulder before stopping at a charcoal-painted door with no number on it. She slid in the card, opened it without ceremony, and vanished inside.

Marti paused at the threshold, the heavy door closing behind her with a soft click that sealed off the outside world. Amber lighting washed over burgundy velvet, the warm glow catching on polished surfaces. Mirrors hung at calculated angles. Enough to create voyeuristic possibilities without the vulgar exposure of a peep show. She breathed in, nostrils flaring at the scent of perfume, liquor, and arousal.

Leather benches curved into intimate clusters. Fabric panels hung between some space. Drawn for privacy in some areas, deliberately left open in others. A silent invitation.

She moved deeper into the room, following Mure's beautiful ass, pulse quickening.

Against the exposed brick wall to her left, a woman pressed her partner backward, fingers tangled in dark hair. The woman's mouth opened in a silent gasp, eyes half-closed. Marti looked away, then found herself looking back.

Through gauze curtains, shadows merged and separated. Three bodies, maybe four. The thin fabric transformed them into living art, all fluid motion and negative space. The low bass of the music seemed to guide their rhythm.

In another alcove, a woman in a red dress traced slow circles on her partner's chest. Her fingernail left faint white lines that faded on dark skin. Others watched from their seats, some leaning forward with undisguised interest, others affecting casual indifference while stealing glances.

No one performed here. That was what struck Marti hardest. These weren't exhibitionists putting on a show; they simply existed in their desire, unconcerned with judgment. The room operated by unspoken rules: watch if invited, approach if welcomed, respect above all.

"What do you think?" Athena asked as she pulled back a drape to reveal their playroom.

"Let's fuck her," Athena said to Mure. "I'm already wet."

Mure kissed and fondled Marti, who let out a low moan. Behind them, Athena watched. She stepped closer to Mure and confidently unzipped her dress. The fabric obeyed, rustling like leaves as it slid delicately down her form, pooling at her feet. Without missing a beat, Mure nimbly kicked away the fallen garment. She was wearing a black bustier adorned with intricate lace and matching fiery red panties.

Athena, with an electrifying touch, latched onto the waist of Marti's tight jeans, whirling her around in one swift movement. Their eyes met and locked, a wild fire stoking between them. Athena leisurely unzipped Marti's jeans, causing Marti to catch her breath.

Standing close by, Mure joined in on the tantalizing torture. With a naughty smirk playing at the corners of her lips, she reached forward to ease Marti's pants past her hips. Strong hands deftly guided her jeans down to pool around her ankles.

An adventuring hand–Marti couldn't tell whose–slipped its way up the inside of her thigh. Fingernails scraped lightly against the sensitive skin there. A shock of pleasure raced up her spine and made her knee buckle. She caught herself just in time, a throaty gasp spilling from her lips as the heat between them continued to rise. "Let me," Marti said as she reached around for the zipper on Athena's dress. Athena slapped her hand away.

"Use your teeth," she said as she turned around. Marti lifted the pull with her tongue and held it between her teeth. As she bent down, unzipping the dress, Mure pulled her underwear down and ran a quick tongue up the crack of her ass. Below her, Marti could see people watching, and it made her wetter.

Mure stepped back, her eyes wide as Athena's dress cascaded to the floor. There it lay in a pool of soft silk beneath her feet, its brilliant hues dancing under the room's soft lighting. Athena bent down and picked it up, letting the cool fabric run through her fingers before carelessly lobbing it onto a clear plastic chair nearby; it landed with a gentle swish.

"Lie down," Athena said, guiding Marti to a particular spot on the floor. "On your side. That's it, lift your leg."

Marti lifted her leg, and Mure deftly guided it through a looped strap, jostling Marti. She gave a quick tug that shifted gravity itself, causing Marti's leg to rise higher in an almost balletic lift.

Athena, her fingers dancing with anticipation, delved into her bag of beguiling toys and emerged with a sleek, leather gag. "Hold up," Marti interjected, her voice hoarse with desire. "I want to taste. Blindfold me instead with..." Her hungry eyes sparkled as she suggested, "Panties?" Her heart hammered at the audacious request.

Waving her closer, Athena snaked her hand down Mure's body to slide off her red panties. The fabric was still warm and moist from her arousal.

Marti parted her hungry lips in preparation. With a soft moan of delight, Athena gradually tied the intimate garment around Marti's head, covering her eyes. An electric shock of desire pulsed through their bodies, elevating the already palpable sexual tension between them.

Marti wondered for a brief moment whether getting into a threesome in a club was the best way to try to find Andreas and Isabella. Marti was sprawled out, one leg idly swinging from the strap. It positioned her to allow observers from other rooms an uninhibited view of the wet skin on her thigh. She casually slipped one arm under her head as if preparing for a nap. This was a great way to get fucked, she decided.

Chapter 6

Athena went down on her like it was her job. Marti flinched at the first swipe of her tongue. Fast, no warning, and let the surprise roll through her. Behind her, Mure shoved her ass cheeks apart, blunt and unapologetic. A knot twisted in her gut. Not fear exactly. Just not knowing what the hell came next.

She tensed, breath catching. The room was too bright. Her skin prickled.

Athena's tongue pushed deep, confident. Marti gasped, gripping the edge of something: sanity, the sink, didn't matter. Mure pushed her face in harder. Marti didn't stop her.

Mure wasn't shy. She kissed and bit down Marti's backside like she was ravenous. The sounds she made were low and messy, humming against Marti's skin as she fucked her with her tongue.

Athena stayed focused. Lips wrapped tight around Marti's clit, tongue flicking like she meant to wear it out. Every lick pulled another breath from Marti's lungs.

Then Athena broke away, rifled through her bag, dumped toys onto the floor like a thief in a hurry.

She held up two: one thick, one narrow. "Slow and steady or fast and rough?"

Marti couldn't see, blindfolded and buzzed. But her voice was clear: "Fast."

Athena grinned. "You got it." She slicked the toys, handed one to Mure, and grabbed Marti's hips.

She kissed her. Not soft. Not sweet. Just wet and direct, tongue forcing its way in.

Then Athena bit her nipple, sucked it like she meant to bruise it. Marti moaned. Athena didn't stop. She dragged her mouth across Marti's chest, biting again. Her hands roamed like she was being frisked. Thumbs rough, fingers digging.

The room stank of sweat and lube and need.

Marti grunted as Athena found her clit again, mouthing it hard and sloppy. Mure lined up the other toy, pushed it into Marti's ass with no ceremony. Marti yelped, twisted, hips fighting the tension until it turned into heat. Her back arched. Her breath punched out in short, sharp bursts.

They moved together: one on her cunt, one in her ass. Bodies slapping. Hands grabbing. She couldn't tell where one ended and the other began.

She grabbed Athena's head, forced her face down harder. "More," she rasped. "Harder."

Mure picked up the rhythm, fucking her with deep, clean strokes. Athena clamped her mouth tight around Marti's clit and didn't let go.

Marti moved with the pull of the strap around her leg, grinding into their mouths and hands like she could climb her way up out of her skin. Her whole body vibrated, chasing the edge. A bite on her shoulder sent her over.

She came loud, voice cracking. Nobody slowed down.

The room didn't smell like sex. It smelled like desperation, sweat, and a fight to stay in control. And Marti wasn't sure she won.

As Marti writhed between them she thought she heard voices whispering from the alcove to her left. Laughter? A woman calling out "Andre?"

Her breath caught. Not just because Athena bit down again, but because she wondered if she heard Andre or Andreas. Did that mean he was close? Maybe even watching?

Marti tried to turn her head, but Mure was already on her. One hand held the toy, the other wrapped firmly against her him. Mure used her body to push in slow, no fanfare, just pressure and heat. Marti gasped, her whole body jerking tight.

Up front, Athena didn't wait. Her own toy slid in smooth, deep, purposeful, like she knew exactly where to aim. The pressure filled Marti quick, robbed her of breath, locked her spine in place.

Mure moaned loud, rough around the edges. It wasn't a performance. She sounded half-feral, and it echoed off the walls like a threat. Her hips slammed forward again, the wet slap of plastic and flesh marking time. She bit down on Marti's shoulder, then her neck, sharp, hard kisses that left no room for guessing she wanted to come.

Athena's moans were lower, throatier. She stayed on Marti's clit, working her tongue in tight circles, relentless. The room was a mess of noise. Wet sounds, breathless gasps, groans that came from somewhere deep.

Marti tried to hang on. She failed. Every thrust dragged a grunt out of her. Every lick had her twitching, chasing it. She rocked with them, forward and back, trying to meet both sides at once.

Athena bit down on her clit just enough to hurt. Marti bucked. The pain lit her nerves like a live wire.

Words spilled out of her in a rush. Curses, demands, names. She didn't care who heard. Her whole body felt like it was vibrating, every inch aching for more. Sweat slicked her back, her thighs, the floor.

Athena and Mure didn't let up. The rhythm was tight, unrelenting. Toys plunged deep, hit her just right. Tongue and silicone and teeth all working her like they meant to wring her dry.

When she came, it hit her hard. Full-body spasm. Eyes clamped shut. The sound she made was more growl than moan. She felt herself spill, felt Athena still latched on like she didn't intend to miss a drop.

Her cheek hit the floor. Her mouth hung open. Saliva pooled beneath her. She didn't care.

Athena pulled back, slow. The toy came out slick. Mure eased off, her pace finally dropping until she stopped.

Fingers unclipped the strap. Marti's leg dropped limply to the floor. Her thighs came together, and the sudden emptiness ached worse than the fullness.

She didn't move. Couldn't.

She just lay there, trying to remember how to breathe.

Athena rolled Marti onto her back and kissed her. Her face was still wet, and Marti took in some of her own juices. She could finally see. And hear.

That goddamned woman laughing again. She needed to get the fuck up. Just as soon as her legs weren't jelly. She walked over and pulled back a drape, certain the laughter had come from there. Not Isabella. A thirty-something goth chick pulling some guy out of his latex dress.

Athena and Mure made out while Marti recovered. Marti was dressing when the door opened. A large man strode in. "Ladies!" he boomed.

"James!" Mure shouted. "Come join us, honey."

James strode confidently in, his power and confidence on full display. His broad shoulders and hairy arms were sun kissed and wide open for a hug.

Marti smiled hazily but was already collecting herself. "I'm just leaving," Marti said as she finished dressing.

"Are you sure, Marti?" Athena asked as she sat up.

"Oh god yes. I don't think I will walk right for a week as it is," she laughed. "Have at it," she said to James. "Everyone enjoy." Inside, gears were moving.

Marti slipped out as two more people walked in, passing them by with a curt nod. She still needed to find Andreas and Isabella, but wrestled with the fact she had no way to document it. No phone, no camera, not even pen and paper. Marti decided she needed to be methodical in her search, whether or not she could record anything right now.

Finding her way back to the desk, Marti started at the first door. Like James, she walked in without knocking. Unlike James, she wasn't there to fuck. Not anymore. The Katsaros's were not there, and she used the opportunity to check the adjacent rooms. No luck.

Marti went door to door, looking past curtains and hoping she wouldn't be kicked out for being so fucking obvious. Up, down, side, side. No Katsaros's. Another room, and she saw a woman in bondage with a ball gag in her mouth. It looked like Isabella, but Marti had to be certain. It meant walking right up to the woman.

Marti walked past the line of people—she wasn't sure if they were waiting to hold or feel the whip—and got as close as she dared. The whip cracked next to her ear, startling Marti. She could see the birthmark. Marti withdrew her face to avoid the next whip flick.

Close.

Fucker.

Marti went back to the reception area, retrieved her things, and bought a ticket to get back in. She slowly made her way to her car, exhausted and sore, and drove home for a good night's sleep.

Chapter 7

The next morning, Marti arrived at the office and sunk into a chair opposite Lori. With some delight, Marti told Lori about the evening at the sex club. She noticed the flush in Lori's skin as she described how Athena and Mure had fucked her.

"Why didn't you just hang out in front of The Sophet? Get some photos? Something we could use for the client?" Lori asked.

Marti lit a cigarette and thought about it for a moment. "Hmm, hang around outside in the rain, or have sex. Hmm, rainy cold street or hot sex club. Street? Sex? Gee, which one should I choose?" she mocked, weighing her hands up and down.

Lori laughed. "Jerk. Look at this," she said, reaching into her desk drawer and pulling out a box. She opened it up and pulled out a small case. Inside were two earrings. "This is the most amazing thing. I bought it last week."

"Earrings?"

"CamLobe. Camera earrings. Check this out," Lori said, pulling them out of the charging case. "The right earring is a tiny camera, and the left one has the shutter button and a nano SD card for saving photos. All you have to do is give a little squeeze, and it captures photos. Very discreet."

"What the hell?" Marti said as she turned the tiny earrings over in her hand. "Wow. So clip them on and..." Marti clipped the earrings onto her ears and squeezed the left earring. A whisper of a click tickled Marti's ear. "Okay, now what?"

Lori held out her hand. "Give it here. The case is the charger and the transfer station. I'll load it onto the computer." Lori put the earrings in the case and turned to her computer. In a few seconds, she looked at a high-quality photograph of herself looking at Marti. She turned the monitor, and Marti gave a low whistle of appreciation.

"Now that's some sweet spy gear," Marti said. "Why don't we have more stuff like this?"

Lori glared at her boss. "We spend most of our money on medical aid. And you keep dipping into the business account to buy Shadow."

"Well, it is my business," Marti said.

"And I have to pay the bills. It's difficult when the account has $10,000 less than I thought," Lori countered.

"But the bills get paid, right?"

"Yes, they get paid. And I get my increase every year, plus bonus," Lori said.

"I give you a raise and a bonus every year?" Marti asked.

"Yes, and you are very generous," Lori said with a grin.

"Shit. Okay, charge the earrings up. I'll go back tonight, get some photos. Want to come?" Marti asked.

"Yes, but not like that. I'll have them ready for you in an hour," Lori said as she turned her monitor back around and focused on the screen.

Marti went into her office, opened the window for a cool breeze, and took a drink or three.

For what seemed like an eternity, Marti had sprawled out on the vintage, worn-out couch. It was only when a peculiar tightness gripped her chest that she stirred from her languor. As she tried to move, hoping for relief, the uncomfortable contraction worsened instead.

Her chest constricted tighter and tighter with each passing second. She struggled to reposition herself, but the pressure in made it nearly impossible. Finally, with a deep breath, she forced her eyes open and jolted upright, startling the cat that had been curled up on her chest. Panic surged through her as she realized her shirt was soaking wet. "What the hell?" Marti gasped, frantically wiping at her face while trying to catch her breath.

Lori rushed in. "What happened?" she asked as she looked around for the source of Marti's distress.

"That fucking cat of yours. I guess it came in through the window and decided my chest was a great place to sleep and get warm. Damn! I thought I was having a heart attack," Marti grumbled as she stood up.

"Bertha is not my cat. You won't let me have her," Lori said. "It seems she's your cat now."

"No animals in the office," Marti said.

"You're the one who broke the rule. Now that you're sober, what kind of update can I give Henrick on his parents?" Lori asked.

Marti shook her head and lit a cigarette. "There's something I don't like about this. We found his parents easily. A simple call to the cab company, and we found their new hotel."

"Maybe Henrick doesn't have cab connections," Lori said.

"Maybe. But there's an end game we haven't seen yet. Trust me." Marti took a long drag and let the smoke billow from her mouth as she spoke. "We should tell him most of the truth. I have seen both Andreas and Isabella. They seemed fine. I wasn't able to take a clear photograph. If he asks where, on a street in Falls City. They were going somewhere, but there was no public access. Ask if he wants us to continue tailing them."

Lori headed into her office to call Henrick, and Marti poured a whiskey. She enjoyed the calm, the tranquility it brought.

Marti flicked through the news on a holo-tab: grand larceny, drug charges stacking like poker chips, a half-burned car ditched after a shootout, two overdoses, and one quiet body found behind a rival's club. Just another fucking day in Falls City.

She tossed the holo-tab aside and put her head on her desk.

"Henrick would like photographic proof. He wants more than one photograph in more than one spot," Lori announced. Her presence roused Marti from her stupor.

"More than one location?" Marti asked as she lit a cigarette. She stubbed out one that was already burning in the ashtray.

"Yes. He didn't take the update very well, and said he was very concerned about their well-being. He said you should have followed them into the building," Lori said.

"There! That's it. He wants sex shots, something to bully or blackmail his parents with," Marti said.

Lori sat down in a chair. "Why not just ask for...Oh, yeah. I guess asking for photographs of your parents having sex is a little creepy."

"Even for me. So, he wants more shots, I'll give him some. I'll go back to The Sophet with a telephoto. No, the CamLobes. I'll get some nice clear images. If they walk down the street, that's a second location. Although I don't know how good Isabella is going to look today," Marti said. "She's going to be pretty sore, from what I saw."

"And yet look at you, able to walk and talk and everything. Listen, we have a client coming in twenty minutes. Another missing person case," Lori said as she rose from the chair.

"We do a lot of that these days. Okay, let me know when she's here. Oh, and bring those earrings in, please."

Marti turned her attention to the computer and searched for more information on the glass sex club. She reviewed the property tax database, but the address on Link Street was owned by a company called Blue Cottage Real Estate. She also checked the address for The Sophet.

"Here are the earrings," Lori said, putting the case on Marti's desk.

"The company that owns The Sophet hotel also owns the sex club building," Marti said.

"Does the company own anything else on the street?" Lori asked.

Marti picked up the earring case and opened it. "Find that out for me, would you? Blue Cottage Real Estate." Marti put the earrings on. "How do I look?"

"I've always said you look great," Lori offered. "Blue Cottage Real Estate. Nothing very cottage-like about a boutique hotel or a sex club in Falls City. Give me five minutes."

In six minutes, Marti was standing over Lori, alternately looking at the computer and Lori's cleavage. "Blue Cottage is owned by Habendum, which, you guessed it, is controlled by Andreas Katsaros. He is President and CEO."

"He heads up GenoHealth, and is also into real estate? And he's staying at his own property, but not telling his son where he is. Why?"

"It was easy to find the information, so it's not like Andreas is hiding it from Henrick," Lori said. "Blue Cottage purchased the sex club building—can we call it something else? The glass house, maybe? Blue Cottage bought the glass house eight months ago. City tax records show it's a warehouse. There were no construction permits issued. I–" Lori stopped speaking when the office door opened.

A young woman walked in. Her brown eyes were wide open, and a smiled grew on her mouth. "Hi? I'm Ria, Ria Preston. I have an appointment," she said.

"Please, come in," Marti said, motioning to the woman to sit. Ria walked into the office and eyed the small chair. She was a large woman with expressive eyes. Marti could see the apprehension on her face. Marti quickly jumped to her feet.

"Let's step into my office," Marti said. She put her hand on Ria's back to guide her. Lori shot a look at Marti, but Marti just winked and followed Ria into the inner office. "Please, have a seat."

Ria settled comfortably into the large leather chair. "Thank you for taking my case," she said.

"I haven't yet."

Marti sat at her desk, surrounded by a haze of cigarette smoke. Her fingers tapped patiently on the surface as she waited for Ria to speak. The woman fidgeted with the edges of the folder in her hands, looking nervous. "My father has gone missing, and I need to find him," she finally said, her voice shaking slightly. "I have some photos of him to help you."

Marti leaned back in her chair, amused by Ria's strange hesitation. She took a long drag from her cigarette before responding. "Don't thank me yet," she said cryptically. "Like I said, I haven't taken the case. So, go on."

Ria paused before speaking again, seemingly hesitant to reveal whatever was on her mind. Marti could practically see the wheels turning in the woman's head as she struggled to come up with the right words.

Finally, Ria let out a deep sigh and spoke. "The thing is…" she began hesitantly.

Marti smirked inwardly. Here it comes, she thought.

Ria continued. "I only have $100. That's all I have. Can you do it for $100? Please? Everyone else has turned me down. One guy even laughed at me."

One hundred dollars was a joke. Marti wanted to laugh too, except this woman—twenty, maybe twenty-one—was shaking. She reminded Marti of a little puppy, and Marti didn't want animals in the office.

"Tell me about your dad," Marti said.

Chapter 8

Marti didn't want another missing person case. They seemed to often end in tragedy. Everything in Falls City ends in tragedy. But here she was, sitting in front of a woman with a missing father and no money.

Ria pulled a photograph out of her folder and handed it over. It was a color photo of the man and a woman, smiling. Oh fuck. Marti stared at it while Ria talked.

"William and my mom, Elizabeth, had been married for twenty-three years," Ria said. "Divorced now, last year. He works in construction. He missed my twentieth birthday, and there's no way he would do that. My birthday was yesterday—"

"Happy birthday," Marti said absent-mindedly. "Lori! Get in here!"

"Does this mean you'll take the case?" Ria asked. Her eyes were hopeful.

Lori stood at the doorway, one eyebrow raised.

"Have you talked to his family members? Parents, siblings?" Marti asked.

Ria told Marti and Lori about William and Elizabeth. His parents died years ago, and he had no siblings. William worked at Xeronia Industries, but when she called the company, they'd refused to speak to her. She'd gone by his apartment and saw his car in the parking lot, but she had no way to get into his home. Her parents divorced after Elizabeth started gambling. They'd never had a lot of money, so the gambling was unforgivable.

"Okay. We're taking Ria's missing father case for $100," Marti told Lori.

"Oh, thank you!" Ria shouted. "Thank you so much."

Lori gave Marti a perplexed look, and opened her mouth to protest. One hundred dollars was chump change. Marti held up the photo of William and Elizabeth, and it silenced Lori immediately.

In the photograph, Andreas Katsaros stood smiling, with his arm around a woman.

"I have more photos. Here's mom and dad at their wedding. Here we are at the fair when I was younger. God, that was fun. Here's me and dad at my graduation..."

Marti held up her hand to silence Ria. "Just give the entire package to Lori. She'll verify your contact information. We will take payment after we find him, not before. Okay?"

Ria teared up. "It's more than okay." After more discussion, Lori gave Ria a form to complete and sent her on her way.

Marti and Lori sat in the office, going over the new Preston case. Lori found an image of Andreas in an online corporate newsletter. She ran facial recognition software on William Preston and Andreas Katsaros.

hey were the same man.

"Marriage records show Andreas married Isabella in 2030 and William married Elizabeth in 2032. Henrick was born in 2031, and had a sister, Katrina, born in 2033. Ria was born in 2035," Lori said.

"Jesus, stop," Marti said. "All these numbers are giving me a headache. You're saying Andreas is a bigamist."

"Yes, a longtime bigamist. One family in near poverty according to the information Ria gave us, one family, multimillionaires. There's no record of William outside of the marriage. No work records, no tax records."

Marti rolled her eyes. "What a mess. We don't even have photographs of Andreas and Isabella for Henrick. And we can't tell him about Ria, nor Ria about Henrick."

She leaned back, frowning. "It's almost elegant. He used his money to erase the poor family, scrubbed them right out of the system. No paper trail, no questions. If they'd been the rich ones, someone would've noticed."

"Why can't they know about each other? Don't they deserve to know?" Lori asked. It incensed her that the two-timing Andreas was treating one family much worse than the other. He'd destroyed lives.

"Ha! Nobody hired us to find half-siblings, they hired us to locate parents. We can't cross that privacy line," Marti said. "I need to go back and get photographs."

"You're going back to the sex club?" Lori asked.

"Honestly, I think my crotch would rather I get photos of them outside The Sophet. She needs a rest," Marti said as she tapped her groin. "I'm going to use the earring camera things. In the meantime, find out as much as you can about Andreas and William. And their wives. And kids. Henrick might have had an inkling and wanted us to find him with the other family. Call him and ask if he has heard from his parents. Maybe it will trip him up."

Marti slipped the earrings onto her earlobes. Pulling the worn leather jacket over her hoodie, she traced the rough patches, symbolic scars etched by time and hardship. The familiar tangy scent of old leather mixed with cheap tobacco lingered around her as she headed out.

Her drive was short but felt long. As she pulled into The Sophet parking lot on Link Street, the ritzy hotel's elegance seemed to sneer at her. She found an unassuming spot beside the hotel where she could blend in with the background. She was just another inconsequential piece of humanity swallowed by the urban sprawl.

A cigarette perched between her supple lips was less about addiction and more about a futile defiance against… she wasn't sure what. It was her minor rebellion under the indifferent sky, a lighthouse amidst an ocean of inaction. Stakeouts are a fucking bore.

Tediousness hung heavy on her like a ghost from an uninspiring past. She kicked aimlessly at the dirt beneath her worn-out boots. Her restless eyes scanned the monochrome sky for variety, for a sign of change, any hint of a silver lining that seemed as elusive as happiness itself.

The sun was setting. Rich people in their gleaming cars were being dropped off down the street, each one a universe away from Marti. Their chatter, coated with privilege and wealth, trickled down to Marti's ears. Disjointed symphonies were foreign, yet fascinating.

But Marti quickly withdrew from these transient distractions, returning to her boots, now smeared with dirt. Her toe dug deeper into the earth—each grain under it whispered tales of broken dreams and second chances.

A pair of black high heels walked up and stopped just inches from her Docs. Marti looked up slowly, taking in the beautiful legs and the tight red dress.

"I saw you at the club yesterday," she said.

Marti looked up. It was Isabella. Behind her, Andreas. Marti smiled. Fuck! Had they made her? She rubbed her earlobe nervously.

"I remember you. You came for a visit, but you didn't stay. At least, not with me," Isabella said.

"There was a lot going on," Marti said with a smile.

Isabella reached out, grabbed Marti's face, and kissed her. "I want those lips, on these lips," she said, looking down.

Marti's smile brightened even more. There was no way she was going to screw a client's mother. "I'm sorry, but I have a commitment for tonight."

"I get what I want. And I want," she said, reaching under her dress, "for my lips..." she said as she withdrew a glistening finger, "to meet your lips." Isabella sliced her finger along Marti's lips, giving her just a taste. "Call your commitment. Break a heart. Come and feast on me." She walked away. Over her shoulder, she added, "And wear the jacket."

Marti's gaze lingered on Isabella as she strutted away, her every move a performance. Andreas was there suddenly, offering an arm, his smirk seeming almost dismissive. "Joining us?" he asked in his soft velvet night voice.

"No," Marti responded quickly, the taste of regret already forming in her mouth. She wished she'd stayed in the damned car. "I've got something else going on."

"Isabella won't be thrilled," said Andreas with a sigh. His soft tone didn't match the hard look in his eyes.

"I mean, I can't...not tonight." Her response hung in the air between them.

"So you're not fond of my wife's taste?" He let the words tumble like a game of chance.

Marti rolled her cigarette in her fingers and mustered the courage to respond clearly; crisp, just like Isabella's lingering perfume. "She's amazing–she has a great taste."

Andreas's features hardened into a storm–each crease on his face, a stab of paint etched against the canvas of his unspoken disappointment. His voice dropped to an uneasy murmur, causing goosebumps to ripple across Marti's skin. "Maybe you're not getting it yet. This place? It's mine. And this street? I run it." The whispering echo of his words danced around them, leaving a lingering note in the air that tasted bitter like poison and smelled faintly metallic. Perhaps a hint of gunpowder and dark secrets.

He arrogantly waved his hand, pointing towards the city's bright lights. "I claim ownership of this street," he declared. "Everything and everyone here is mine."

Two figures standing as silent sentinels caught Marti's eye. One was almost hidden behind a translucent window-pane in The Sophet, chiseled by moonlight. Another was secluded under a tree's canopy, whose rain-bitten leaves barely concealed firearms in hand.

"Got it?" Andreas's question was rhetorical but demanding all at once, both territorial yet unfeeling. The men watched silently.

"Let me see what I can do," Marti said. Pleading was subtle but the tension palpable as she pulled out her phone, ready to dial the office number. Andreas wordlessly nodded, his face was hard, cruel. "Hey, it's me. Remember that gift you got me?" Marti asked.

"I didn't get you a gift," Lori said.

"I'm wearing them right now."

"Oh, the earrings. They aren't a gift. What about them?" Lori asked.

"How do I, uh, how do I..."

"Marti Starova, you are never at a loss for wo—" Lori stopped. "Can you talk?"

"No."

"It's about the earrings?"

"Yes," Marti said.

"You need to…Take a picture? Transmit?" Lori asked.

Marti looked at Andreas. "Yes, mistress."

"Mistress? What th—Ugh. Never mind. Okay, on your phone, tap the CamLobe app. Do you see it?" Lori asked. "Open it and hold the phone to your left ear. It will connect and transmit the images."

Marti pulled the phone away from her ear and flipped through the apps. She looked at Andreas and mouthed, "I'm being tracked." He nodded. Marti tapped the CamLobe app and held the phone up to her ear. "Yes, mistress, I did as you said. Yes, no. Yes I can. No, I am waiting here as I was told."

"Okay, I have nineteen images. They… yes, they look good. Our couple. Are you there with them?" Lori asked.

"Two then one. Yes, mistress, as you say." Marti hung up the phone. "I'm sorry," she repeated. "I have a commitment. But if I can put a word in with her when she arrives, I will let her know about your wife's interest."

"Yes, she's very interested, so I am very interested. And you can't come now?" Andreas asked.

Marti shook her head.

"Then give me your jacket. It will give her a chance to smell you while I fuck her. That will hold her over for a while," he said.

Marti shook her head. "No, my ja—"

When Andreas casually flicked his wrist and his stooges began advancing on them like creeping shadows, she recognized trouble. Marti shut her mouth. Goosebumps prickled her skin as the looming threat bore down on her like a rogue wave. She hastily emptied her pockets. Cigarettes, phone, a lighter, her inhaler. A couple of receipts she had to turn in to Lori. Strains of scraping metal echoed in her ears as she fervently unzipped her leather jacket. Its familiar, comforting smell wafted into her nostrils. Marti surrendered it to the crew.

She watched traces of dust dance in the harsh traffic light. There was movement somewhere. This, she thought, would not end well.

Andreas was happy and left with a smile and a wink. The thugs on the sidelines went back to doing nothing, and Marti stood, shivering in the cold.

Chapter 9

Marti called Lori back and explained that while she was standing outside The Sophet, Andreas and Isabella approached her. At first, she thought they made her as a private detective. It became clear that they wanted her to join them for sex.

"Are you going in?" Lori asked.

"God no. Send the images to Henrick. Let him know his parents are fine. Close this fucking case," Marti said. "It's creeping me out."

"It's got to be bad when you're creeped out. Okay, I'll take care of it. You have a good night. I'm going home after this," Lori said.

"Me too," Marti said.

Marti stood for a few moments, watching people walking down the street. Like moths to a flame, they were drawn to the sex club. They would only sate their hungers and desires in the company of strangers. A wave of acrid exhaust, mingling with musky perfume and raw want, floated from the cars that ferried them. It stung her nostrils. Her stomach twisted in desire to yield to these same lusts.

As she turned away, Marti thought she saw something moving out of the corner of her eye. She spun around, heart racing, but there was nothing there. Just the street and people who draped their desires around themselves like veils.

Fingers trembling slightly, she fished out her inhaler; its metallic coolness offering an illusion of control. It was the wrong time and the wrong place, but that never stopped her. She inhaled Shadow deeply into her lungs, each molecule bringing a peculiar comfort that enveloped her.

Finding solace on the cold, damp curb, she sat down; a silent observer watching a theater of hidden desires unfold on this strange stage in front of her. Anticipation settled within her as she questioned what hunger would next be exposed; what naked truth it would drag out from under its cloak under the comforting canopy of darkness.

Gradually she let herself melt into the scene like a silhouette merging into the darkness, waiting. With a frightening allure, she looked towards whatever it might reveal. She was Marti Starova...and yet at this moment, she barely knew who Marti was.

Marti shivered in the chilly air, her feet numb and aching from sitting too long. Finally, mustering up enough energy to leave, she started walking up the street, towards her car parked at The Sophet. Just as she was almost there, an ear-piercing siren erupted from the club behind her.

She froze in place, watching people scramble out of the doors in a chaotic panic. Some raced blindly ahead, desperate to get away, while others wandered aimlessly about in confusion. The fear radiating off the frenzied crowd was palpable even from a distance, but Marti stayed rooted to the spot, unable to move or look away.

She strained, trying to spot the Katsaros couple go by, but she couldn't see them for the flood of bodies. She couldn't quite shake the effects of Shadow. Its effects were becoming unpredictable and sometimes, terrifying. Bodies merged, molten movements of flesh and fear. Marti turned to walk away, and was stopped in her tracks.

A stream of red and blue flashing lights came from both ends of the street. Tires screeched as car after car pulled up. Big black cars, a van, another van. A flood of paramilitary personnel rolled over the area. Helmeted police wore tactical ballistic vests and carried compact submachine guns. Inducement Rejoinder laser dazzlers flashed across the area, blinding and disorienting people trying to flee.

"Get down on the ground, get down on the ground!" They weren't Falls City cops. "Get down on the fucking ground or I'll shoot you!" Marti got down on the fucking ground. She spread out and waited as boots stormed around her. There were shouts and buzzy radio voices and overwhelming commands for people to obey. A helicopter circled overhead and more transport vans arrived.

Someone yanked Marti to her feet. A large gloved hand had Marti by the back of the neck, pushing her toward a newly arrived van. He slammed her against the side of the van. She was roughly searched, wallet taken, handcuffed, and forced into a small cell in the van. With only a small slit to look out, Marti watched as more people, mostly naked, were put into vans and cars and taken away.

It made no sense that they raided the club; sex wasn't illegal.

The rear door of the van opened, flooding her dark cell with light. Someone looked in. "Are you Martina Starova?" The woman's voice was demanding. She shone a bright flashlight into the cell, and compared Marti's face to the identification taken from her when she was searched.

"Yes," Marti said.

The door unlocked, and Marti stood up.

"Sit down!" the woman yelled, and Marti sat down.

"I am Agent Heather Blair with the Federal Unified Crime Taskforce. You're under arrested for possession of a controlled substance, to wit, Shadow," she said.

"Fucking Shadow," Marti mumbled. "What's going on?"

"Did you not just hear me?" Heather asked.

"I meant everything else," Marti said. No one was arrested for possession of an inhaler anymore, not in Falls City. There were millions of dollars in drugs flowing through the streets of the city. A minor bust like this was just a way to keep someone in jail.

"None of your business," Heather said. She shoved Marti's wallet and cigarettes into her hoodie pocket and slammed the door shut. Marti knew something bigger was happening. There were two loud bangs, a signal to leave. The van engine roared to life, and she was driven away.

The jail was ten miles away, and Marti was nervous. As a former cop, she hated the idea that she'd be locked up even for a short period. She hated the handcuffs; she hated the van. She hated it all.

"Fuck this," Marti grumbled as she kicked the wall. She squirmed around, pushing her hands under her butt and then down her legs. She stepped through and brought her cuffed hands in front of her. It was much more comfortable. She searched her pocket. It didn't surprise her to find she had no lighter.

The van turned, then turned again. Soon they slowed and then stopped, then started again. Marti looked out and saw chain link fencing and razor wire. She was inside the Falls City Jail holding area. Every fiber of her being told her to kick whoever opened the door, to head butt her way out and run. But they would shoot her, probably kill her.

The door opened and Marti climbed out of the van. "You look familiar. You've been here before?" the guard asked as he guided her inside to the processing area.

"I have one of those kinds of faces," Marti said. She looked up at the six-storey building with a new perspective. Where once she had seen the strength of justice, Marti now saw the darkness of corruption.

She knew she would be allowed to make a phone call soon enough. She just had to bide her time. The sound of metal doors slamming open and slamming shut sent echoes through her head. "Stand here," a guard barked. Marti stood there, a neutral look on her face.

"Go there," he said, pointing to a bench. "Boots, belt, hoodie off. Put them in the bag." Marti put everything into the clear plastic bag she'd been given. She put on foam slippers and shuffled to the next set of chairs.

More than a dozen women sat waiting. On the wall, a grimy phone was the focus of Marti's attention. She didn't know Lori's home number. She didn't know anyone's phone number, except the office. Marti stood in line for her turn to make a phone call.

A shiver went down Marti's spine; she felt like she was being watched. She looked around. One woman was smiling at her, two women were glaring at each other, and everyone else had their heads down. Marti looked at the woman staring at her. Marti nodded. It was Naomi, the woman she had met recently while working another case.

It was Marti's turn to use the phone. She wiped the earpiece off on her jeans and dialed the office. "Lori, it's Marti," she began when the beep indicated it was being recorded. "I'm at Falls City Jail. Get me the fuck out." She hung up.

The holding cell reeked of industrial disinfectant trying to mask piss and desperation. Marti sat on the metal bench, her back against the cinderblock wall that leaked cold through her thin shirt. Two cells down, someone was crying. Had been for the last three hours. The fluorescent lights hummed their migraine song.

"Psst. Name's Aubree. What's yours?"

"Marti. Got smokes?"

"Nah. Got Shadow."

Abree pressed against the bars between their cells, her face gaunt in the harsh light. The trustee had that look, the one that said she'd figured out how to work every angle in this shithole.

"Not interested," Marti said, though her hands were already starting that familiar tremor. Seven hours since her last hit. She'd been counting.

"Come on. I know you're hurting." Aubree pulled something from her waistband: a slim inhaler, medical-grade. "One hit. That's all I got left anyway."

Marti's mouth went dry. "What do you want for it?"

"Your clothes." Aubree's eyes traveled down Marti's body, clinical as a coroner. "Socks, underwear, bra. Mine got stolen in the showers."

"Fuck off."

"Suit yourself." Aubree started to turn away.

The tremor spread up Marti's arms. In six hours, she'd be out. Six hours was nothing. Six hours was forever. Down the hall, the crying stopped, replaced by someone screaming about spiders.

"Wait."

Aubree smiled like she'd already known how this would go.

Marti stripped in the corner, back to the camera, movements mechanical. The concrete floor was sticky under her bare feet. She passed the clothes through the bars. At least she'd still have pants and a shirt when they released her.

The inhaler was warm from Aubree's body heat. Marti turned it over, checking the gauge. One dose left, just like promised.

"Enjoy the ride," Aubree said, already pulling on Marti's bra.

Marti retreated to her bench, cradling the inhaler. The metal was smooth, familiar. How many times had she done this? Hundreds? Thousands? She pressed it to her lips and inhaled.

The Shadow slid down her throat like watered whiskey. Wrong.

Not stronger or weaker, just... diluted. Like someone had cut it with something that didn't quite match.

She waited for the warmth, the blessed numbness that would smooth the edges off everything. Instead, the world just shifted sideways a few degrees. The screaming from two cells down sounded like whale song. The fluorescent hum became a swarm of electric bees.

But her mind stayed sharp. Too sharp.

Kane's face surfaced first. That sanctimonious fuck with his perfect conviction rate and his corruption so deep he stopped being human years ago. Dead now, along with Rufus Montgomery, the IT weasel who'd helped Kane set her up.

Five years ago. Charlie Gomes in interrogation. Gomes escaping. Sabrina Kogoya, twelve years old, found with her chest carved open, her heart missing.

Marti's fault. Always her fault. Except—

The thought hit like cold water: I didn't let him go.

She'd carried that weight for five years, let it eat her from the inside, fed it with Shadow to keep it manageable. But Kane let him escape. Kane set her up, hired Rufus to fuck with the interrogation room video.

In reality, not her fault.

The guilt that usually crushed her chest was... gone. Just gone. Like a tooth finally pulled after years of agony, leaving only the weird absence where pain used to live.

"So what the fuck am I doing this for?"

Her voice echoed off the walls. Down the hall, someone laughed, harsh and manic.

She looked at the empty inhaler in her hand. All those hits, all those years of dulling a pain that wasn't even hers to carry. The Shadow wasn't working because there was nothing left to numb.

She lay back on the bench, the metal cold against her bare skin. The jail sounds washed over her: toilets flushing, guards gossiping, someone beating a rhythm on their cell door. Usually, Shadow turned it all into white noise. Now each sound stood distinct, real, impossible to ignore.

But for the first time in years, the chaos didn't claw at her. She closed her eyes and let it become a lullaby of sorts. Sleep came easier than it had any right to, there in that stinking box with its symphony of human misery. Maybe because for once, she wasn't running from anything.

The Shadow had shown her the truth: the monster she'd been hiding from had never been hers at all.

Chapter 10

Marti couldn't believe it: busted for drugs, but no one else in holding looked like part of the sex raids. She sat there, watching the rats claw each other inside the cages. She was one of them, and they all knew it.

She scanned for someone familiar. Naomi caught her eye, gave her a short nod. Marti moved.

Naomi sat calm in the middle row, oversized coat draped over her lap. She didn't smile when Marti approached, just shifted and opened a little space.

"Naomi, right?"

"You remember."

Marti's voice dropped. "All of you."

They'd crossed paths before. Some intel had been exchanged, a pity fuck in an alley after. Naomi had done the fingering that time. Now she raised an eyebrow.

"Wanna return the favor?"

"Here?" Marti glanced around. Guards didn't seem to care, not really.

"No one's looking."

Naomi leaned back, legs parting slightly under the coat.

"Right or left-handed?"

"Right."

"Switch sides."

Marti sat. Her hand disappeared beneath the coat like it was routine. Skin, then heat. No buildup. She pressed two fingers in through damp fabric, then under it. Naomi's breath caught.

No kissing, no words. Marti moved with quiet, practiced intent, sliding inside, circling once, then again. Naomi's thighs flexed, her coat shifted slightly, but no one turned their head.

A cough, low and guttural, was the only sound Naomi made. Her hips jerked, barely controlled. Marti's fingers curled, hit the mark, and stayed there.

Movement. A guard.

Marti pulled out fast. Naomi adjusted her coat. Marti kept her eyes forward.

The guard stopped. Looked. "Everything alright?"

"Yes, sir," Marti said, her tone blank.

He watched too long, then moved on. They waited, still as corpses, until his steps faded.

Naomi's hand slid over and squeezed Marti's thigh.

Marti didn't ask permission this time. Her hand disappeared again. The scent hit first. She moved quicker now, thumb on Naomi's clit, two fingers thrusting deep.

Naomi's head tilted back. One hand over her mouth. Her body jerked, then froze. Marti felt the pulsing, the wetness, the grip of thighs going tight. She didn't stop until Naomi shuddered out the end of it.

Marti pulled her hand back, wiped her fingers on the inside of Naomi's coat. She sucked one clean.

"That was something," Naomi muttered, breathless, slipping her underwear back in place.

"Location, location, location," Marti replied, flat.

"We need to stop meeting like this."

Marti sniffed her fingers. "Do we?"

"Stop staring!"

The shout came from down the row. A blonde woman glared at her partner like she wanted blood.

Marti leaned back. The show, apparently, wasn't over.

A wicked smirk slowly bloomed across the brunette's face as she leaned just that little bit closer, casting waves of contemptuous heat in her wake. "I'm not looking at you. 'Cause seriously," she taunted, her voice tinged with an almost savage pleasure. "You're so fucking ugly, it's criminal." She scanned the room for any signs of interference, but saw nothing. The guards sat still behind their desks. "You'd look better with my fist in your face," she added with venomous glee. She figured he hand towards the blonde who responded with a slap.

Seated several rows away from this fiery showdown, sat Marti and Naomi, who watched the scene unfolding. Both fighters seemed to thrive amidst turmoil more than anything else; their harsh words and erratic actions were quite revealing: drug users in the throes of coming down. She noticed how much more restless and on-edge the blonde appeared compared to her opponent. There was an unsettling dynamic energy simmering beneath her skin that was hard to ignore.

As if on cue, the otherwise hushed air split wide open when the blonde launched herself toward the brunette without warning. A swift, straight kick aimed stirred up such intensity within seconds that its palpable tension spread around them like an approaching thunderstorm. The fight gathered momentum, fast hands flailed through the air from both women.

The blonde channeled all her pent-up rage into a clean stroke; her hand flew smoothly yet ferociously like a primed whip. The loud smack that followed was starkly clear even amidst the booming chaos echoing off walls. Finding herself a sudden target, the brunette let out a pained yelp. Shaking it off quickly enough, she rallied and hit back, hand slicing through air to meet its mark like a rattlesnake going in for its kill.

Taking a cue from the escalating scene, guards jolted into action from behind their desks and rushed toward the impromptu arena. They encircled both women, closing in on one another, spurred further by eager cheers of encouragement.

"What fuckers," Marti spat.

Chapter 11

This was her chance to prove her usefulness to Marti. In case she didn't already know.

Lori walked up the boulevard, enjoying the respite from the rain. She had her umbrella, but used it as a walking stick rather than a protector. She was strolling up Violet Gardens Boulevard, a lovely hillside street off 156th Street. There were two bookstores she had to check.

It was morning, and she wanted to get an early start. Instead of heading into the office, she had gone directly from home. There was no point in wasting the dry weather.

Tracking down Katarina Katsaros hadn't been easy. Lori couldn't find an address or phone number. Fortunately, she was on social media. A lot of selfies in Finnigan's Flake, a pastry shop on Violet Gardens, but she was always eating, sitting at a table. She was a customer there.

Katarina also posted photos of herself in a bookstore, in various sections on various days. Lori guessed it was where she worked. The bookstore would have been near the pastry shop, and voila! Two bookstores.

The first bookstore was on the west side of the street. It was a large retail store offering stationary, bookmarks and greeting cards on the first floor, with a mass of magazines in the corner. Lori loved the place. It was a real throwback. She wandered upstairs and looked around the shelves. It just didn't look like the right place. With a quick scan of faces, Lori headed to the next store a block north.

This one was an independent bookstore, one of the few remaining in the entire state. It was three floors in a narrow building, maybe only twenty feet across. Once you threw in jammed bookshelves and piles of hardbacks stacked on the floor, it felt like she'd walked into the home of a literary hoarder. This was the place.

The store emanated a nostalgic charm. The air was thick with the musty scent of well-worn paper, a fragrance that lingered as a testament to decades of literary exploration. Bright, warm lighting cast a soft glow on shelves that reached to the ceiling, their wooden surfaces showcasing an eclectic array of aging books. Dust particles floated in the air despite the damp weather. The sight was a haphazard mosaic of literature, both good and bad.

There were two customers–browsers, really–and one employee. Katarina, who sat behind a tall desk, was reading. She wasn't at all what her photos on social media showed. There, she was bold and brash and funny. Here, she was quiet and mousy and reserved. She looked up to see Lori staring at her. She said nothing.

"Hi." Lori said.

Katarina waited for a moment and replied, "Hi. Is there something you are looking for?" Her voice was pinched and high.

"Yes, you," Lori said.

"Ah, another social media devotee. I do not do girls."

"Thanks for that tidbit, but I'm not here for that. You're Katarina, right? I want to say I'm sorry for your loss," Lori said.

Katarina leaned back and looked over her glasses, sizing Lori up. "Like I said, I do not do girls."

"I'm here about your father. I have some questions."

Katarina stood up and came around the desk to fully take in Lori. She made no bones about looking at her carefully from toe tips to crown. "Are you one of daddy's whores?"

"Will it get me some answers?"

"No."

"Then no, I've never actually met your father. I work with a private investigator. We're following up on a few things after his passing," Lori said.

"Murder, you mean," Katarina said as she leaned back against a bookcase. "I am sure you meant to say his murder. Do you know who did it?"

"No."

"You are not very good at investigating, are you?" Katarina asked.

"Well, I like to think I'm very good. I found you and I'm guessing the cops haven't."

Katarina tilted her head. "You interest me. In an annoying way. Ask any questions you want. But just know, you may not like the answers."

"Tell me about your father," Lori said. It was vague.

"You are not my therapist. Try again," Katarina said.

"You asked if I was his whore. One of his whores. What can you tell me about his whores?" Lori hoped this was clear-cut.

Katarina pushed herself off the bookcase and walked to the front door. She looked out, across the street and up the street. "He has a lot of them. Some are more popular than others, I think. I cannot tell you any names, although I am sure my mother could. One woman, early twenties, medium height, fattish. She is his favorite. Was. The opposite of my mother. He even brought her to the house one day, though I have no idea what he thought that would accomplish. The girl made it out alive, nonetheless. So it all worked out in the end," she said. "It is raining again."

Lori raised her arm. "Good thing I have my umbrella. Did any of your father's mistresses have–"

"Not mistresses. Don't glorify them. They were whores. All of them."

At least one of them was a wife, Lori thought. It was clear Katarina didn't know about Elizabeth. "Did your father have any women in his life who hated him?"

Katarina laughed and reached out for a book on the shelf. It was a thick hardback, heavy and well bound. It would hurt if you got it in the head. "I hated him, for one. But I did not kill him. I know that is your primary question. The next question, I was working here when he died. We stay open until midnight. The third question will be, 'did any of his whores want to kill him?' Only one I can think of. He set up shop with her in a little place over on Lexford Avenue. Bought the building and let her open her dream business," Katarina said. There was bitterness unbefitting her fairy voice. "A yoga studio, I think. It is called All Yoga. Something like that. That might be a good clue for you, detective."

Lori smiled. "Yes, indeed. What's with the animosity? I barely know you, but you seem to have taken a real hate to me."

Katarina took the heavy book back to her side of the counter. "I was fifteen when my father kicked me out of the house. He said I read too much. Can you believe it? He said, 'Katarina, these books are putting bad ideas in your head.' He gave me a thousand dollars and the back of his hand." Subconsciously, Katarina touched her cheek.

"I do not care that he is dead. I do not care that you are investigating that troll's death. He was a vile, perverted man and I will not miss him one bit." With that, Katarina opened the large book and began to read. Intently. Dismissively.

As Lori turned to leave, Katarina said, "Wait." She reached under the counter and pulled out a slim volume. "Didion. 'The Year of Magical Thinking.' About grief and loss. Not that I'm grieving him, but..." She shrugged. "You look like someone who appreciates good writing."

Lori took the book, surprised by the gesture. "Thanks. I do."

"It's used. Five dollars."

Lori smiled and handed over a five. Not charity after all. But as she slipped the book into her bag, she noticed

Katarina had tucked a business card inside with a phone number scrawled on the back.

"If you find out who did it," Katarina said quietly, "I'd like to send them flowers."

Lori thanked her and left. She threw up her umbrella and headed for the car. She had parked it a block away, closer to the larger bookstore. Lori hadn't come across that kind of hostility in a long while. Katarina hated her father, and there was venom in her words. Lori tumbled into the car, folding the umbrella as she slipped inside. She tossed it on the passenger's side seat and pulled out her phone.

After writing a quick summary of her interview with Katarina, Lori looked for the address for All Yoga, but there was no such place. With a little more sleuthing, Lori found Olive's Yoga, which sounded close to "All Yoga". It was 156 Lexford, half a city away. She sighed, started the car, and drove off, listening to the GPS system give her the wrong directions. The forty-minute drive took an hour and a half.

Lori found a parking spot right outside the studio. It looked empty save for a young woman sitting in a lotus position on the floor. The rain drummed hard on the windshield and bounced off the hood. She made a dash into the yoga studio and flicked water onto the floor as she stood inside the door.

Chapter 12

Lori stood inside the yoga studio, taking in the scents of fresh lemon and sweat. Her conversation with Andreas's angry daughter had given her nothing but this. It was good enough. "Hi there," Lori said to the seated woman. She opened her eyes and smiled.

"Hi. You're a little early. I start the next class in thirty minutes," she said as she rose gracefully to her feet. She was young and lithe and barely contained by the spandex. Watching her move was like watching water flow. Why would Katarina call her 'fattish'?

"My name is Lori Harring. Are you Olive?"

"I am. Hi Lori. Are you here for a single session? Or were you hoping to sign up?" Olive asked as she stretched and arched and flexed.

Lori looked around. There were no other people. "I'm here about Andreas. I'm sorry for your loss."

Olive froze mid-pose for a moment, then continued the cat-like stretch. "Yeah, he was a nice man. Set me up here, invested in my business, you know?"

"That's very kind. Did he come here to see you in action?"

Olive eyes her warily. "Who are you again?"

"My name is Lori. My firm is working with his family." It was a mostly true statement.

"And what brought you here?"

Lori hesitated for a moment. "Katarina."

"Ah, yes. I've met her. I've met the whole family."

"I never had the pleasure. If you don't mind me asking, will you be okay without his ongoing investment?"

Olive laughed. "You're nosy. And funny, I like that. Come and sit," she said, gesturing to a cube on the floor. "Andreas was a great guy. Lots of fun. He bought the building and gave me a thirty-year lease on the place for a dollar a year. Studio and the apartment above. That doesn't change now that he's gone."

"That's a really generous thing," Lori said.

"Would you like some tea? Organic herbal mint, to brighten the mind," Olive said. She turned the kettle on and pulled out two small glass tea cups.

"Mint sounds delicious," Lori said. "I'm looking for a bit of background on Andreas. He was an interesting man."

"I'll say. He was a gentleman, in case you're wondering. He was married and very loyal to his wife. I know how it must look, but I should say, we never slept together or anything." Olive said as she poured water into the cups and dunked the tea bags in.

"Thank you for telling me that. I'd heard the opposite, so I appreciate the clarity," Lori said as she took the teacup from Olive. The glass cup gave off fragrant aromas, a refreshing tang tinged with a subtle sweetness. Wisps of steam rose from the cup, carrying with them the calming essence of fresh mint leaves. Through the clear glass, Lori saw liquid jewels in hues of amber, with vibrant mint leaves dancing gracefully within.

"You've been talking to Isabella, haven't you?"

"You knew he was married?"

"Of course, I said I did. He never lied about that. Look, you seem like a pretty open type of person. So I'll tell you, I had an affair with him. I lied earlier. I mean, he's dead now, so he won't mind if I tell anyone. He was into some things that, well, needed me to be very flexible. Andreas's solution was for me to become a yoga instructor. Make some money, learn some new positions. Honestly, he was a lot of fun," Olive said.

Lori wondered why Olive had at first lied about her relationship with him. "So you miss him?"

"Yeah, of course. He...Look, he had a lot of women and as far as I know, he was always a pretty decent guy about it. There's a lot to miss, you know?" Olive said.

Lori nodded. "Any idea who might want to hurt him?"

Olive took a sip of tea and shook her head. "His daughter. Katherine, I think. She hated his guts. She runs a bookstore over on Violet Gardens Boulevard. You should talk to her."

"I did. She sent me here. And I'm sorry to have to ask this, but where were you when Andreas died?"

"At home with my boyfriend. I saw the raid on TV, but I didn't know Andreas was caught up in it. I mean, it was sad, but it sure looked exciting on the TV," Olive said. "Do you think the cops killed him? By accident? During the raid?"

"No, I don't think so. Thank you for your time. I'll let you go so you have a little time before your next class. Thanks for the tea." Lori headed back to her car and watched Olive's Yoga for a while. She saw dark figures dash from awning to awning and then into the studio.

Once inside, each person invariably threw off their coats, unrolled their yoga mats, and began twisting.

Lori sighed. It had been a waste of time, but at least that was another thing off the to-do list for Andreas.

After her meeting with Olive, Lori sat in her car, organizing her notes. She couldn't help but think about Katarina. The bitterness, the trauma. The bookstore seemed like both a sanctuary and a prison for her. Lori made a note to send her an anonymous gift card to Katarina at Finnigan's Flake. It wouldn't heal old wounds, but perhaps a small kindness might matter. She also jotted down "Potential witness if needed" but suspected Katarina would sooner burn down the police station than cooperate officially.

She finished her notes and drove back to the office.

Once at her desk, Lori listened to the voicemail message and cursed. Gathering her things, she headed out to rescue Marti from jail. Again.

The mid-morning sun shone brightly in Marti's eyes. "What the hell?" Marti said as she stumbled through the exit and into the parking lot.

"It's called sunshine, Marti. Surely you haven't forgotten already. You were only locked up for a night," Lori joked.

"Yeah. Thanks for bailing me out," Marti said.

"I cannot tell you how shocked I was to pick up that voicemail this morning. Why didn't you call me at home?" Lori asked as she approached the car. "Are you driving, or me?"

Marti fell against the car, holding on to keep herself upright while the world spun around her. Lori laughed and wrapped an arm around Marti's shoulders.

She opened the door for Marti and shoved her gently in, closing it behind her with the snick of metal on metal.

"You drive, I'm too tired," Marti said. It only just registered that Lori had already made that decision for her. She let out a sigh of relief.

Climbing into the driver's seat, Lori said, "Too much noise for you to sleep?"

Marti lit a cigarette and took a long, luxurious drag. "Sex and fighting."

The car engine rumbled to life. "You got into a fight?"

"Not me. I had sex. Someone else got into a fight."

Lori turned onto the street and looked at Marti. "Of course. Was that with that woman you wanted to bail out? Oh, do you want coffee or breakfast?"

"Yes, please," Marti said, exhaling a cloud of smoke. She opened the window, needing to get something resembling fresh air. "Yeah, Naomi. I thought she'd want to get bailed out, but she decided to stay. At least until the police turf war ends."

"What do you want for breakfast? Sit down or take out?"

"Sit down, I guess. Let's park at the office and hit that little place around the corner, the coffee shop," Marti said. She watched the city as they drove through. It somehow seemed a little different this morning. "Oh wait, stop here, just for a second," Marti said as they approached the entry to Kransten Park.

"Really?" Lori asked. "Didn't you just get busted for drugs?"

"I know, weird, huh? Yes, here. I need a hit." Lori pulled over and watched as Marti exited the car.

Marti jogged into the park, eager to find a dealer and buy an inhaler. She walked toward the fountain where she would normally find her man. Someone new was waiting, hands in pockets, near the bench. He smiled and stared at Marti as she walked past him. He was too new and seemed to be too eager.

Marti strolled around the park. She saw four new dealers. None of the regulars were there, and all the other junkies hanging around looked nervous. Everyone was trying to decide who they could trust. Marti was certain the answer was 'no one.' She headed back to the car.

"All the dealers are gone," Marti said as she got inside.

Lori pulled away. "There are no drug dealers in Kransten Park?" Lori asked. "I don't believe it for a second."

"There are dealers. They just aren't the regular ones. It must be the Feds. They're stupid enough to think that arresting every dealer and sending in their own undercover agents is a good idea. I don't think anyone was buying," Marti said. "Take a right up here. Stop."

Lori turned right and stopped. Marti hopped out, not even bothering to shut the door behind her. She ran down an alley; the puddles splashing up under her feet. "Hey," she said to a man in the shadows.

"Hey Marti. Good to see a familiar face," he said. "What the fuck is up?"

"I need some Shadow. And you tell me what the fuck is up. I just went to Kransten Park, and something weird is going on," Marti said. She dug into her pocket and stepped further into the doorway. Tommy followed behind.

"A couple of the big labs got burned down. No one wants to start up a new lab until they know what the fuck is going on," he said.

Marti laughed to herself. She'd burned down one of them by accident and the other was burned down by the owner to rid himself of a couple of troublesome cops.

"They investigating that?" Marti asked as nonchalantly as she could.

"The fuck would I know? How much money do you have?"

"Huh? Why?" Marti asked warily.

Tommy looked over his shoulder. "Huge busts means fewer street level supplies. You know that. Price has gone up. But this shit is pure. It's a crisp," he said.

"What the fuck? It was $100 yesterday. How the fuck is it $1,000 today?" she snapped.

"Because it is. Come on Marti, that's the going price. Decide fast. I want to get out of here," he said. He shifted from side to side and looked around. Something spooked him. "I have ten to sell."

"Gotta take credit," she said as she tapped her wrist device and held it out. Tommy held out his wrist, and she tapped the reader. It buzzed slightly, letting him know he'd just received $10,000. With one last glance around, he handed Marti a plastic bag full of inhalers and walked away. Marti shoved it into her hoodie and rushed in the opposite direction. She had to backtrack to get back to the car.

"Fuck me," Marti said as she sat down next to Lori.

"I've been trying," Lori joked.

Marti looked at her with a grin. "You really have. And the answer is still no. I meant, the price of inhalers has gone up ten times. Ten times! If this isn't temporary, like really temporary, the shit is going to hit the streets. You are going to have some really desperate junkies out there looking for a lot of money."

"A thousand dollars for one of those? You really need to scale it back," Lori chided as they pulled into the parking lot. Marti quickly stashed nine inhalers under the seat and opened one. She took a long hit and let her head fall back.

"So good," Marti said.

Chapter 13

It wasn't good. Not fucking good at all.

The cracked vinyl seat dug into Marti's spine as she waited, muscles tense. Nothing. By now that electric fizz should have been crawling up her vertebrae, making the world shimmer and dance. Instead, her eyelids sagged like they'd been sewn with lead thread.

Between her fingers, a small inhaler rolled back and forth. Shit. Tommy had leaned in close, breath hot against her ear: "This shit is pure." His eyes had gleamed with the confidence of a man who believed his own bullshit. Yet here she sat, blood turned to cold syrup, every heartbeat an effort.

"You good?" Lori's voice cut through the fog.

Marti grunted, not ready to admit the truth. Outside their crawling vehicle, Falls City decomposed in real time. Sunlight knifed through the windshield, highlighting Lori's white-knuckled grip on the wheel. They inched past another dead storefront: plywood where windows should be, spray-painted warnings fading under layers of grime.

"Tommy's full of shit," Marti finally mumbled, tongue thick and uncooperative. "This shit is garbage."

Between abandoned cars, a man with hollow cheeks shuffled aimlessly, his shadow stretching across asphalt split with weeds. No repair crews in this part of town, not for a decade at least.

Marti's fingers twitched along the seat edge, toward where she'd thrown her other inhalers. A cold sweat broke across her forehead.

A siren wailed somewhere beyond the maze of collapsed overpasses and dead-end streets, rising then fading like everything else in Falls City. Marti pressed her palms against her eyes, willing the Shadow to kick in, to deliver that blessed floating numbness that made existence here something close to bearable.

Her body remained stubbornly, painfully present.

Across the street, a billboard peeled away in long strips, revealing its rusted skeleton beneath faded promises of better living. Marti watched it disintegrate, a mirror to her insides.

"Maybe," she whispered, more to herself than to Lori, "it's time for something stronger."

The words felt heavy in the stale air. Her head tilted back against the headrest, and the rhythm of Lori's driving—stop, crawl, stop—became a lullaby. The broken city blurred past her window, and despite everything, her eyes finally surrendered to the weight they'd been carrying.

A notion popped into her head that she should look around. When she opened her eyes, Lori was already halfway down the block. She'd left the keys on Marti's lap. Marti jumped out, locked the car, and jogged after Lori. "I'm getting a workout today," she said as she caught up, following Lori into the café.

"I don't quite get it," Marti said. "What happened last night? I didn't have any access to the news."

"I'm not sure. One large coffee, black. One red spice latte, hold the sugar. Two croissants, please. I heard nothing on the news. Except there was some kind of raid or something last night. There is supposed to be a press conference about it today," Lori said. She paid for the drinks. "I'll find a table. You get the drinks," she said as she walked away. Marti made a face: there were no other customers, so every seat was empty. When the coffees and pastries were ready, Marti brought them to the table and sat down.

"So, where were you this morning?"

"I was checking out Henrick's sister, Katarina. And she led me to Olive," Lori said. She sipped her latte.

"Olive? Who's Olive?"

"The other reindeer."

Marti stopped mid-bite and stared. "The what?"

"The other reindeer. Olive the other reindeer. Geez, were you ever a child?"

"Nope, came out of my father's head, fully formed. I don't think I have your home number," Marti said, turning on her phone. "I was going to call you, but I have no idea what your number is. Can I put it in my phone?"

"Sure, but are you going—"

Marti's phone rang: it was a number she did not recognize. "Hello?"

"I'd like to speak with Martina Starova," the woman said.

"I think lots of people want to speak with her," Marti said, throwing Lori a sideways glance. "Who are you?"

"Agent Heather Blair with the Federal Unified Crime Taskforce. Is this Martina Starova?" Heather asked. She sounded impatient, but Marti felt like playing a game with that jerk from last night.

"Well," Marti said as she took a bite of croissant and chewed noisily into the phone. Lori smiled and raised her eyebrows, and Marti winked at her. "What would a federal agent want with her?"

"That's a concern for Martina," Heather said.

"It's raining now," Marti said. "Is it raining where you are?" She loudly took a sip of coffee. "Sorry, can you repeat that? I didn't hear you. The rain is loud."

"I said, what has rain got to do with anything?" Heather asked.

Marti took another bite of croissant and smacked her lips. "Golly, just trying to be friendly with a federal agent," she said.

"Cut the crap. Is this Starova?"

"Such offensive language," Marti said with faux shock. "That's not nice language for a federal agent. If that's who you really are."

"Oh, for the love of...Martina Starova needs to attend the Falls City police headquarters within an hour, or she'll be arrested. Heather Blair. Tell her to ask for Heather Blair," she said and hung up.

Marti looked at her phone. "Demanding woman," she joked. "I don't trust her. This Heather Blair is the one who arrested me yesterday outside the sex club. She was directing a lot of arrests. She'll arrest me in an hour if I don't go see her. Let's head back to the office, get our shit together."

"Such offensive language," Lori said with faux shock and a laugh.

A ringing phone greeted the women as they walked into the office. Lori opened her desk drawer to see which one was ringing. "Henrick's burner," Lori said, answering the phone. "Hello? Hello?" She looked at the phone. "Huh. He hung up."

"That's not—"

The door didn't just open, it slammed against the wall hard enough to rattle the frame. Henrick stumbled through like he'd been running for blocks, phone clutched in his white-knuckled fist, chest heaving.

"What happened to my dad?" The words came out as a roar that made both women freeze. He lunged toward Lori's desk, knocking over a coffee cup, sending papers scattering.

Marti shot to her feet, hands up. "Jesus Christ, Henrick—"

"You were supposed to keep him safe!" He was close enough now that she could see the broken blood vessels in his eyes, smell the stale sweat and panic rolling off him. "He's DEAD! Someone killed him and you—" His voice cracked, going from rage to something raw and broken. "You were supposed to protect him!"

"No, you didn't hire me to protect him. You hired me to find him. And I did. Alive and well."

Henrick's face twisted. "Alive and well?" He let out a sound somewhere between a laugh and a sob. "ALIVE AND WELL?" He swept his arm across Marti's desk, sending everything crashing to the floor. "He's in the fucking morgue!"

Then, as suddenly as the rage hit, it drained out of him. His knees buckled and he caught himself on the edge of the desk, shoulders shaking. "I'm sorry, I... God, I'm sorry. Someone killed him last night."

"You found him just in time for someone to kill him! If you hadn't led them right to him—"

"Stop right there," Marti's voice went ice cold.

"No! You don't get to 'stop' anything anymore! I PAID you. And now he's dead because you couldn't do your fucking job!"

Henrick's shirt was buttoned wrong. His hair stuck up in the back like he'd been pulling at it. There was a coffee stain down his front and his hands wouldn't stop shaking. Not just trembling, but violent, uncontrollable shakes that made his keys jingle in his pocket.

"I found him for you," Marti said. "I sent proof he was okay."

When he collapsed in the chair, something shifted in his eyes. The wild panic was still there, but underneath it was something colder. More dangerous.

Marti lowered her hands, slowly, carefully. "I was in jail last night. Unrelated to your case. Lori, show him my bail receipt."

Henrick waved his hand. "You don't need to."

"You need to see for yourself," Lori said as she held out the paper. "Seriously. Put your mind at ease about it. One less thing to worry about."

Henrick cradled the paper in his hands as if it were a wounded bird, acknowledging its contents with a slight nod before returning it to Lori. Marti sparked up another cigarette, filling the quiet space between them with the stinging scent of burning tobacco. Her voice barely rose above the ensuing smoke when she asked, "And your mom? Is she alright?"

He swallowed hard before answering. His mother, always in his heart. "Yes," he muttered tersely. His gaze seemed lost in a distant thought as he added, "She was there with him...at some nightclub."

The ambient noise dimmed as Marti took an anxious drag from her cigarette. A silence so thick that even her throat-clearing seemed to echo around them. They were both piecing together the grim picture painted by his words.

"They were dancing, living it up," Henrick continued, his voice wavering for the first time in their conversation, "and then he got stabbed." His eyes met Marti's, fraught with fear and uncertainty. "Mom didn't even see who did it."

Marti nodded. She was pretty sure they weren't dancing. "Stabbed?" Marti asked.

"In the chest. I...I'm sorry about getting angry. I just don't know what..."

"No worries," Marti said. She looked quickly at the time. She had twenty minutes to get to police headquarters. "Lori, send Henrick every photo I took, even the blurry ones. I'm sorry for your loss, Henrick. I need to go talk to the cop who arrested me, but you can stay with Lori until you're okay to leave," Marti said.

"Why were you arrested?" he asked.

"Drugs," Marti said, tossing a Shadow inhaler onto Lori's desk. "Sorry, but I have to go."

Chapter 14

Marti resented the call from the Federal Agent, demanding she attend an interview. Heather Blair was a fucking bitch, Marti thought as she climbed into her car, the leather seats cracked and the engine reluctant to turn over. She eased out of the crowded parking lot and onto the road, taking a moment to admire the shiny red sports car in front of her. Suddenly, blaring horns pierced through the peaceful hum of the engine. The aggressive driver behind her leaned on their horn for what felt like an eternity, stirring up a surge of anger within Marti. The loud noise grated against her ears, and she was ready to snap.

As the red light bathed the street in its glow, the driver of the car next to Marti's pulled up alongside her. She was a woman with long, golden blonde hair, heavily painted with makeup that seemed to try too hard. With an air of entitlement, she rolled down her window and screamed at Marti, shaking her finger and unleashing a torrent of curses before abruptly pulling away as soon as the light changed. Marti could almost feel the weight of the woman's contempt hanging in the air after she had gone.

"Fuck that." Marti let the car get ahead, but then followed a few cars behind. She knew she had less than twenty minutes before she was arrested, but she was going to handle this her way.

With a quick jerk of the wheel, Marti pulled over to the side of the road to watch the blonde woman park on the street. Her sleek, expensive car glided into its spot with ease. Once the woman was gone, Marti smoothly pulled out and headed towards her target. With calculated precision, she maneuvered her car along the side of the woman's vehicle, relishing in the loud screeching of metal against metal. It was a symphony to Marti's ears, filling her with a twisted sense of satisfaction. With a devious smirk, she stepped on the gas and sped off into the distance, leaving behind a trail of exhaust and distressed metal behind her. She was going to have to get her car fixed.

But right now, she needed Lori.

"I did some digging," Lori said on the phone.

Marti threw her cigarette out the car window. "So Andreas is dead?"

"Yes. Last night. News reports don't list a cause of death and they are pretty tight-lipped about the location. It just says it was downtown Falls City," Lori said.

Without much of a thought to it, Marti gave a finger to City Hall as she passed by. It was there. It deserved it.

"I'm almost at headquarters. Is there anything about my jacket?" Marti asked.

"No," Lori said. "Nothing about clothing. Maybe that's what Agent Blair wants to talk to you. About Andreas."

Marti turned into the police parking lot. "Maybe. The Feds were clearly set up for a raid, but we don't know if he was dead before they arrived, or if they killed him. Okay, I'm here. If I don't call you in an hour, call me. If I don't answer, come find me. The fuckers might detain me again. Oh, and find me a list of cheap car repair shops. I got dinged."

Once inside, they escorted Marti to an interview room. She didn't have to wait long for Heather Blair to show up. She was a striking woman with fiery, long red hair that flowed gracefully down her back. Marti wondered how she got it all under the helmet she was wearing when they first met.

Heather's green eyes locked onto Marti as she walked in. "I'm Agent Blair, with the Federal Unified Crime Task-force."

"FUCT. Funny," Marti said. "Who came up with that name?"

"Your drug charges are not a joke, Ms. Starova," she said as she sat down.

"Call me Marti," she said, extending her hand.

Heather's face softened. Marti knew the tactic. "Heather, call me Heather. When they arrested you, you had a Shadow inhaler in your possession. What brought you to that area?"

"I had no drugs on me. Mind if I smoke?" Marti's fingers moved with ease as she reached for her pack of cigarettes, the plastic crinkling under her touch. She flicked open a lighter and let out a long drag of smoke, exhaling a cloud that hung heavy in the air.

Heather watched with narrowed eyes, trying to mask her curiosity with a patient, neutral look. But Marti knew better. Heather was like a fox, cunning and sly, desperate for any shred of information. But little did she know, she was dealing with a wolf.

"Okay, what were you doing on Link Street?" Heather asked.

Marti knew where Heather was going with the questions. The Feds had clearly been staking out the sex club, they would have seen everything. Heather was hoping for a lie, a wedge that she could drag into the open to exploit. "I was walking back to my car a few blocks away. I think I got a parking ticket on it. I'm sure you can check."

Heather's head tilted to the side, mimicking Marti's stance. To counteract this, Marti reclined in her chair and stretched out her legs, making it nearly impossible for anyone to mirror without drawing attention. They filled the room with tension as the two women engaged in a subtle standoff, each trying to assert their dominance through body language. It was a battle of wills, and neither was willing to back down. Marti liked it.

"I'll get someone on the parking ticket," Heather said with a smile. Marti hoped it was killing her to be this nice.

"Oh no, I'm not asking you to fix my parking ticket. That's dishonest," Marti said, waving her hand.

"That's not what I meant," Heather said. "I meant, have someone verify the time and date of the ticket." Marti had just established miscommunication between them, something she could point to later if need be.

"Where were you coming from?"

Marti knew Heather had most of the answers already. There was no point in lying. "I was trying to find a woman's father at The Sophet hotel. While I was standing there, I talked to a couple for a while. And left." Marti blew smoke from her nose and licked her lips. Heather was an objectively attractive woman. Marti wondered if she was in to women.

"What woman hired you? What couple did you speak to?" Heather asked.

Marti spoke in a low, gravelly voice, her words laced with mystery and intrigue. The words tumbled out of her mouth, each one carefully chosen. "I am a private investigator," Marti stated with a hint of authority. She couldn't reveal the identity of her client or the person she was searching for; it was part of her code. "I can't tell you who hired me, or who I was looking for. And the couple I spoke to never gave me their name," Marti said. All true.

As she talked, Marti expertly rolled a cigarette between her fingers, her focus on the task at hand as if it held all the answers she sought. The smoke from her cigarette swirled and danced in the dimly lit room, creating an air of clandestine urgency.

Heather was diligently writing notes on a notepad. It was a quaint style of personal note keeping. The interview was being recorded, as it always was, and the computer would transcribe everything said. But some cops liked to carry around notepads, like it gave them some form of legitimacy. "What did you talk about? With the couple," Heather asked.

Marti stared at Heather's breasts for a moment, watching her breathe in and out. They were cute. On the small side. Marti guessed her areolas were dark, maybe an inch and a half wide. Heather shifted her body, pulling Marti out of her musing.

"They asked if I wanted to join them for the evening. I said 'no'. Repeatedly said 'no'. I'd never met them before, so I declined," Marti said. "The guy asked me for my jacket. Threatened me, honestly. I took my crap, gave him the jacket, and walked away. Thirty feet later, police are everywhere and you arrested me."

Chapter 15

Marti was enjoying her talk with FUCT agent Heather Blair. FUCT was such a glorious name. She had a strong idea this was about the murder and not the drugs.

Marti stubbed her cigarette out and put the butt in her pocket. Heather noted it. It meant nothing. Marti was just playing with her. "Can you describe the jacket?"

"Worn black leather. What has this got to do with my arrest? Or do you have my jacket?"

"We certainly have a jacket. But we'd need your DNA to match to the jacket, to confirm it's yours," Heather said.

"I have to say, I'm surprised you have my jacket. I mean, as crazy as it sounds, I saw a ton of people running around naked. No jackets to be seen. You were there, waiting. You saw all the naked people too."

"What do you recall about that moment?" Heather asked.

"Which moment?"

"When you were at the scene?"

"I recall seeing naked people, and then the police arrested me. Not for being naked, though. I'm not sure what your reasonable cause was," Marti said. She leaned forward and inhaled deeply. She made it obvious not by sucking in air, but by flexing her nostrils. More animalistic.

"We had reasonable cause. We found an inhaler of drugs," Heather said with surety.

A sly smirk curled across Marti's lips, her gaze narrowing as she considered Heather's investigative prowess. The room, bathed in the sterile glow of a desktop lamp, seemed to hold its breath in anticipation. The faint hum of machinery and the distant shuffle of footsteps from the bustling office provided a backdrop to their exchange.

Leaning casually against the worn edge of the desk, Marti's fingers idly traced the outline of a case file, the texture of the paper providing a tactile grounding. Her senses heightened. She inhaled the faint scent of ink and aging paper.

"Procedure is, you can't find something and then say you had reasonable grounds. You have to have reasonable grounds and then find something. You know that," Marti remarked, her voice a low, deliberate cadence that echoed in the confined space. The click of a pen, the subtle shuffle of papers, punctuated the moment, creating a symphony of bureaucratic sounds.

Heather, unfazed but determined, met Marti's gaze with a steadfast resolve. The air between them crackled with unspoken tension. Marti wasn't sure if it was professional or personal. Marti's gaze, a piercing storm of gray, held Heather's steady, as if daring her to unravel the puzzle.

But Heather could do no such thing, and tapped her pen in frustration.

Marti grinned and chuckled. "Let me ask you: are you working with Falls City Police? Or are you siloed?" She was hoping this was a chance to knock Heather off her game. She forced her nostrils wide again, trying to catch the scent of Heather, but the smell wasn't there. It's likely she showered this morning and used a neutral deodorant. Something that would not offend the 'no perfume' policy in the building. Marti shook her head and laughed to herself.

"Something funny?" Heather asked.

"Nah, I'm just a pig sometimes. Makes me laugh. So, working in a unified team with Falls City, are you?"

"That's not really something I can discuss. Would you be willing to provide your DNA so we can match it to your jacket? Possibly get it back to you?" Heather asked. She had a slight smile, but was otherwise neutral.

Clearly no one had told Heather. Marti sat up and leaned forward. She wanted to watch Heather's eyes dilate, her cheeks flush. "I'm a former homicide detective in Falls City. My DNA is on file. Did no one tell you?" Marti delighted when Heather's body reacted to the news. She lit another cigarette. "I'm notorious. Everyone who is anyone knows my name. Chief Franklin would surely have told you."

Heather swallowed hard and set her jaw. "I certainly did not tell Chief Franklin that I arrested a drug user," she said. Marti could tell by her tone she thought calling Marti a drug user would throw her off.

"Drug addict. Not just a user. I'm a drug addict. Or, as some people like to say, a 'substance misuser'. I used to be a homicide detective. The Force has paid for three trips to rehab in the last five years. Gotta love the never-ending health benefits. Yeah, the last case, a little girl with her heart torn out. I just couldn't do it anymore after that one, you know? Have you ever had a case like that? A little girl with her heart ripped out of her chest?" Marti grabbed a handful of air and yanked, mimicking a terrible crime.

The color drained from Heather's face, and she put her notepad down. She was probably getting confirmation through an earpiece right now. Her forehead glistened as her body heated. It was turning Marti on. Marti sniffed again, but despite that, nothing.

"Someone has bailed me out on that mistaken charge of drug possession," Marti said. "So if you don't have any other questions…"

"Who is your drug dealer?" Heather asked, trying to regain her composure.

Marti sighed and took a drag of her cigarette. "No set dealer. I know better. If I don't have a regular dealer, I can never tell you who it is."

"Did you meet your dealer there? Did you meet anyone other than the couple there?" Heather asked. "I'm not trying to jam you up. I just need to cross you off the list."

Ah, Marti thought. Time for the reveal. "What list?"

"Can you confirm if you observed anyone or anything that seemed suspicious in any way? As a homicide detective, you would have a special awareness that only detectives have," Heather said. Now she was trying to play to Marti's ego. Clever.

Marti knew she had to give her something. "Frankly, everyone who was naked was suspicious. So I…Wait. You know what I thought was weird? Yeah. When I was talking to the guy, the one who took my jacket. The reason I gave it to him was he had men. Muscle. One guy watching us from inside The Sophet. Another across the street. I remember, he held his hand out and waved or something. And these guys started moving in. He said they'd take the jacket from me if I didn't hand it over. So he took the jacket, and the guys faded away. He had security with him."

"Why didn't you tell me this earlier?" Heather asked, exasperated.

"You wrongly arrested me for drugs. That's what I thought this conversation was about. Not about a murder I had nothing to do with. That guy had security, and he took—stole—my jacket. He wasn't my dealer. I didn't trade a jacket for drugs," Marti said.

"No. No, that's not...look the man died after talking to you. We're just trying to find out what happened." Heather finally came clean about what she wanted from Marti.

"I was arrested maybe ten minutes after talking to him. I know nothing about his death. If you'd just asked me that, we could have avoided all this. You could have just questioned me about the jacket instead of trying to in-timidate me with a fake drug charge." Marti knew she was being a dick, but her frustration was justified. They had arrested her just after speaking to him, so she knew ab-solutely nothing about his death. If they had simply asked her that question from the start, all of this unnecessary trouble could have been avoided. This chick was a pain in the ass.

Heather shook her head, frustrated. "Okay, alright. You're still being charged with possession."

"I don't really care. It's a false arrest. I didn't have any drugs. And now you're angry at me for not being able to help you with this guy," Marti said. She was setting up yet another defense. Petty revenge of a cop for failing to give up information. Perfect.

"I'm not angry. We're done. Someone will be here in a minute to escort you out," Heather said. She stiffly walked out, trying not to show her anger.

Marti looked at the time. It was an hour and a half, and Lori had not called. Marti was pissed.

Chapter 16

The meeting with Heather was useless. More than useless. Because Marti lost her temper on the way over and rammed another car, it was going to cost her to replace it. She took a quick look at the damage caused by her rash behavior. She ran a finger along the deep grooves and laughed. "Worth it," she said out loud. The worn door of Marti's car groaned in protest as she pushed it open and slammed it shut.

She made the drive back to the office without killing anyone, which was a good sign. Marti's walk up the stairs was not one of casual observance; it was charged with a brewing storm of frustration. Lori should have called. The low shuffle of her footsteps was a stark contrast to the tension that reverberated within her body.

She had left explicit instructions for Lori to call after one hour, yet an hour and a half had slipped by, leaving Marti in the clutches of a federal agent.

As Marti prepared to address her secretary, her nostrils flared, catching a whiff of stale perfume lingering near the office. The sensory details converged, all framing the impending storm as Marti steeled herself for the overdue confrontation with Lori.

Ready to unleash her discontent, Marti opened the door of her office, ready to blast Lori for not calling her.

Marti stepped through the doorway and stopped. Lori was sitting at her desk, smiling and chatting with Ari Stirling. Stirling was a member of one of the large three crime rings in Falls City. He had previously hired Marti to find out who had killed the head of the ring. She would rather not have to deal with Ari Stirling. Ever. For anything.

"Mr. Stirling, good to see you," Marti said as she walked in. They shook hands as Ari stood up.

"Your lovely secretary has been keeping me company. You and I need to talk," Ari said. Marti still found his eyes creepy and his manner narcissistic.

"Lori, thanks. You can go for lunch," Marti said. Lori never went anywhere for lunch, but she was smart and she knew it was time for her to leave the office. Marti was happy to see her pick up on the directive and go.

"Great, back in forty-five," Lori said as she grabbed an umbrella. It was just starting to rain. Lori nodded once as she headed out the door, closing it behind her.

"Ari, what do you want?"

"I understand Henrick Katsaros hired you to find his parents, Andreas and Isabella. You found them. And then, in a strange coincidence, Andreas was murdered," Ari said.

Ari's voice sliced through the air like a dagger, each word laden with a tone for an uneasy conversation. Marti felt the prickle of tension at the nape of her neck, the room's atmosphere morphing into a clandestine theater of revelations.

A frown was etched on Marti's brow, a silent protest at the ominous path this conversation was taking.

"I have nothing to do with his murder. You know that's not my thing, Ari. Never has been," Marti retorted, Marti's fingers, restless, drummed against the arm of her chair.

She wished for the comforting weight of her gun against her hip, a tangible reassurance in the face of accusations veiled in insinuation.

"You were close by," Ari countered.

"And the Feds arrested me within minutes. I didn't–"

"Arrested for what?"

"Drug possession," Marti said. She saw Ari's face and added, "I couldn't believe it either. But I was in jail. I didn't see anything, I didn't hear anything. I'm just getting back from talking with the Federal Agent who arrested me. She was interested in the murder, not so much my drugs," Marti said. "Speaking of which." Marti headed to her desk drawer and opened it. Damn, the inhalers were still in the car.

Ari shifted in his chair. "I hired you some time ago to find out who killed Marcus Thornfield, and you did. Now, I want you to find out who killed Andreas. He was my money man."

"Ah fuck."

"You said that out loud," Ari said.

"Yeah. Sorry. I meant 'dang,'" Marti corrected, her expression marked by a subtle blend of chagrin and amusement. A smirk lingered, a testament to Marti's ability to navigate through linguistic pitfalls with a certain nonchalant finesse. And to just be an ass.

A flicker of movement as Marti lit a cigarette, an intimate ritual that punctuated the unfolding drama. The flame danced briefly, casting fleeting shadows on Marti's features, caught in a momentary interplay of light and smoke. The room was now tinged with the acrid aroma of burning tobacco. "Look, it's really complicated," Marti said.

"What's the matter, Starova? When have you ever shied away from complicated?"

Marti inhaled deeply and blew this smoke out with force. "What can you tell me about Andreas's personal life?"

"Andreas has—had—a wife and a son. And a daughter, I think. He worked for me, and neither of them knew it. He was an honest, stand-up guy. Loyal to a fault. I trusted him with hundreds of millions in assets. I think he collected stamps or some shit," Ari said. "There is nothing in his personal life that caused this. Not even his proclivities got him here. It's me they are after. Someone is trying to fuck with me, and I want them found."

"So you knew about the sex club?" Marti asked.

"Yes, of course. He was killed there. Why? Do you think that had something to do with it?" Ari asked.

Marti stared at him for a moment, deciding if he was joking. He wasn't. "That is where he was killed. It would seem that sex had something to do with it. Could it have been his wife? A bit of jealousy?"

"No. She controlled him, but let him do anything and everything. There was nothing to be jealous of," Ari said.

"Well, there was, actually." Marti thought about Ria, who still did not know that her father was dead. "Fuck, this is going to get messy. Are you sure you don't want to just leave the Feds to handle it?"

He laughed. "No, of course not. They can do their job, but you can do yours. Will you take the case?" Ari asked.

Marti stubbed her cigarette out and nodded her head. "Yeah. But no taking your anger out on me, got it? You're going to find out things you don't like. His family will find out things. You have to guarantee my safety. Nobody comes for me or my secretary."

"Shit. You already know something, don't you? Yes, yes, guaranteed. Trust me, no one will come for you," Ari said.

"No one? No matter the cost?" Marti asked.

"No one. No matter the cost. But that makes me nervous. And don't tell his family I've hired you."

Marti nodded. "Let me get Lori back in here. She'll set up a file," she said, messaging Lori. She also asked her to bring up the inhalers from the car.

"Can I get you a whiskey?" Marti asked. Ari shook his head slowly. "It's like nobody has any vices anymore," she grumbled, her voice heavy with a hint of self-deprecation.

With a sigh, Marti rose from her chair and her footsteps echoed softly against the wooden floor as she made her way to her desk drawer. Her fingers brushed against the cool metal handle, the familiar sensation sending a shiver down her spine.

Inside the drawer, a shot glass and a bottle awaited her. Marti retrieved the glass, its smooth surface cool against her palm, and poured herself a generous measure of whiskey. The amber liquid sloshed gently into the glass, its rich aroma filling the air with a symphony of toasted oak and mellow spice.

Bringing the glass to her lips, Marti took a deep breath, the pungent fumes stinging her nostrils. She tilted her head back and let the fiery liquid slide down her throat, a wave of warmth spreading through her body. The alcohol burned a trail down her esophagus, leaving behind a lingering sensation of comfort.

As the whiskey settled into her system, a sense of calm washed over Marti, easing the knots of tension that had been building within her. The harsh edges of her day softened, replaced by a hazy contentment that lulled her into a state of tranquility.

With a sigh of contentment, Marti set her glass down on the table, the rhythmic ticking of the clock filling the silence. She closed her eyes, savoring the moment of respite, letting the whiskey work its magic.

Ari watched Marti as she nursed her glass of whiskey, her gaze fixed on the amber liquid swirling within its depths. She seemed lost in her thoughts, her lips tracing the rim of the glass with an absent-minded gesture.

Ari glanced at his phone, the screen flashing with unread messages and urgent notifications. The demands of work beckoned.

Without a word, Ari rose from his chair. He cast a fleeting glance at Marti, her eyes still locked on her drink, and then turned and walked out of the office.

The door swung shut behind him, leaving Marti alone in the dimly lit room. She raised her glass to her lips, taking another sip of the whiskey, and smiled. She'd gotten rid of him.

Chapter 17

Lori walked into the office without the inhalers and sat down. Marti had sent her a message to come back to the office and to bring the inhalers. Marti shrugged when she saw Lori's empty hands, and frowned. "Make up a file. We're investigating Andreas Katsaros's death for Mr. Stirling. Get in touch."

Marti started digging around into the cushions of the couch. No inhalers. She rifled through her drawers. No inhalers. She dug through pockets of various hoodies. No inhalers. Finally, Marti petulantly collapsed into her office chair and slowly spun in circles.

Lori walked into Marti's office and leaned against the doorjamb, arms crossed. "The file is set. Ari is gone. Why did you want me out of here?"

"I thought he might kill me. Figured you didn't need to be here for that," Marti said as she brought her chair to a halt. "Where are my inhalers?"

Lori's eyes widened in disbelief, her expression morphing into a mix of amusement and concern. "You thought he was going to kill you? Why?" she asked, her voice laced with skepticism. "Why on earth would Ari even consider harming you?"

Marti shrugged, her lips curling into a sardonic smile. "I don't know," she replied. "I guess it was just a hunch, a feeling that crept up from the depths of my paranoid, drug-addled mind. After all, we've all witnessed his angelic nature, his unwavering kindness and compassion."

Her words dripped with irony, the sharp edges of her sarcasm cutting through the room like a knife. Lori couldn't help but chuckle, the sound echoing through the dimly lit office. "Marti, you're such an Oscar Wilde," she teased.

Marti snorted, her laughter carrying a hint of bitterness. "Well, someone has to keep things interesting around here," she retorted, her gaze drifting towards the window. "Life would be awfully dull if not for people like me."

"Someone is watching the building," Lori said. It made Marti sit up straight. "A redhead. Green eyes. Gorgeous. Sound familiar?"

"Did she have dark areolas? I think that's Heather Blair, the Fed who arrested me. She's got it bad for me," Marti said. "I mean, arresting me for drug possession? Really?"

"That's why I didn't bring your inhalers. When I saw her, I didn't want to get busted," Lori said. "So, what's the Ari case?"

"Finding Andreas's killer. With a promise that no one comes after us, no matter what we uncover. So, first things first. We have to tell Ria that her dad is dead," Marti said.

"This is going to be messy," Lori said.

"Call her. Set up a meeting at her home. We'll bring what we have, let her know William is Andreas, and he is dead. We will get photos, marriage certificates, everything. Gauge the reaction, figure out if maybe she was involved," Marti said.

"What about Heather? Think you can work with a tail?" Lori asked.

"That's a hot little tail, isn't it? I have to figure out a way to use her. It would be great to get access to her level of information," Marti said.

"I don't think even your charms will work. She looked very serious," Lori said.

"I'll take that bet. Let's see...if I can get her to help our investigation–"

"Substantively help our investigation," Lori interjected.

"Substantively help our investigation, then I win. If I can't, you win. What are the stakes?" Marti asked.

Lori laughed. "If I win, I want to take you on a date. An actual date. Dinner, wine, a stroll down the street."

"That sounds so 'teenager,' but okay. And if I win, I want you to...I want you to wash my car. In your underwear," Marti said.

"In my underwear? Who's the teenager now?" Lori laughed. "Deal."

"Alright. Let's get to Ria's place and get this over with." They drove in Marti's car. Lori mocked her for wanting the damaged car to be washed.

"I don't care about the car. I just want to see you working up a sweat." In your underwear, Marti thought.

Chapter 18

Ria and her mother, Elizabeth, sat at the kitchen table. A constant tremor betrayed Elizabeth's fear. She couldn't look up.

Marti took a deep breath. "Things are very complex. But first, before we get into details, let me confirm. This is William Preston?" Lori pulled out a photograph of Andreas taken just before he died.

"Yes, but I don't recognize the suit. William didn't wear suits," Elizabeth said. Ria picked up the photo and frowned.

"What's going on?"

"I'm sorry to say, but William passed away two nights ago."

Elizabeth slipped out of her chair and sat on her knees on the floor. Her mouth was open, her face screwed up in pain, but no noise came out. Ria, on the other hand, sat up straight in her chair and wailed, deeply and loudly and from the depths of her heart.

Lori kneeled beside Elizabeth and put her arm around her shoulder and held her as if to hold in the screams. It didn't work, and the screams came out. They were high pitched and ragged, the opposite of Ria's low, guttural sobs. Marti wanted a hit of Shadow and a smoke. She reached out and put her hand on Ria's. It was the most she could do.

Eventually Elizabeth's sobs became gasps as she finally took in air. Ria's wails became moans as her throat gave out. Marti looked around for a tissue and saw none. She wandered until she found the washroom and brought a roll of toilet paper back to the kitchen. She ripped off a portion of toilet paper for each woman and then ripped off more. They were mostly through the roll by the time both women were back at the table and ready to listen.

Marti didn't wait for them to ask the questions that no wife or daughter should have to ask. "He is the victim of a homicide." Marti waited. No sound came from either woman, and she continued. "I don't know the exact circumstances. I am going to give you the name of the Federal agent investigating the crime."

"Federal agent?" Ria asked.

Marti's composure remained unruffled, despite the gravity of the situation. Her voice, though laced with concern, held an unwavering steadiness as she faced the grieving widow and her daughter. "This isn't easy, and I'm not here to make it worse," she said, meeting their eyes without flinching. "But you deserve the truth, and I've got it. Lori, can you please get the photograph of Isabella?"

Elizabeth paled. Marti showed them the photo. "Do you know this woman?" A gasp escaped Elizabeth's lips, her hand instinctively reaching out to clutch her daughter's arm. Ria's eyes widened, shock flickering across her face. Elizabeth and Ria looked carefully at the image.

"No. Did she...do this?" Ria asked.

"I don't think so. This is Isabella Katsaros. Does her name sound familiar? What about Andreas Katsaros, or their son Henrick? Daughter Katarina?" Marti asked.

"Who are they?" Elizabeth asked. Her voice was suddenly hard.

Fuck. Marti had told dozens of people that their loved ones were dead. Not that their loved ones had another family and another life and that's what got them killed.

Marti cleared her throat. "William was a bigamist. He had a second family. I'm sorry, I know it's hard to believe," Marti said as Ria and Elizabeth immediately objected.

A chorus of protests erupted from Ria and Elizabeth, their voices intertwining in a mix of disbelief and anger. "That's not possible!" Ria exclaimed, her eyes wide with shock.

"He couldn't have been! That's just bullshit!" Elizabeth echoed, her voice shaking with emotion.

Marti reached for Lori's phone and swiped through to a photo of William, holding it up for Ria and Elizabeth to see. In the picture, a man stood smiling beside a woman and kids, their faces beaming with happiness.

"To them," Marti said, "he was Andreas Katsaros."

Ria and Elizabeth exchanged glances, their expressions a mix of anguish and disbelief. Ria's eyes filled with tears, her voice choked with emotion. "How could he do this to us?" she whispered, her words barely audible.

Elizabeth's face hardened, her eyes blazing with anger. "He lied to us," she hissed, her voice laced with bitterness.

"Do they know about us?" Ria asked.

Marti shook her head. "I don't think so. But I will be speaking with them." Marti explained to the stunned women that William led a double life. She produced the Katsaros wedding certificate and other photos provided by

Henrick. Marti said when Ria came in, they were already handling the missing persons case for Henrick. "But of course we had to investigate, to verify they were the same man."

Marti told Ria and Elizabeth she would be in touch with the Federal Agent on their behalf. "And I recommend you hire a lawyer as soon as you can."

"Wait? Why do we need a lawyer?" Ria said. Anger mixed with shock and she gritted her teeth.

"You're going to need two lawyers," Marti said flatly. "One for criminal. One for family court. The Feds aren't going to let this slide. They'll look at you like suspects, because that's what they do. And that other family? They've got money. Serious money. They'll come at you hard for every damn penny of William's estate. You'll need a lawyer who bites, not begs."

Elizabeth's face drained of color. Ria just blinked, stunned.

"We can't afford even one lawyer," Ria said finally, her voice tight. "Not one. Not even close."

Marti nodded once. "Yeah. I figured. You're going to need someone who'll work pro bono, or for a percentage. Maybe someone with a grudge against the wealthy. But they're out there."

Elizabeth looked lost. "I don't even know where to begin."

"Neither do I," Ria said. "We don't know anyone. We're not those kind of people."

"No shit," Marti muttered. "That's half the reason Andreas could vanish you. The system eats people like you and spits out bones."

She turned to Lori. "We'll need names. People who know how to throw a punch in court and aren't scared of going up against a family with a million or two to burn on legal fees."

Lori nodded. "I'll find someone. I know a few who might take the case for the cause."

It took ten more minutes to calm the Prestons down enough to leave them. Marti and Lori stepped out into the cold evening.

"God, that was terrible," Lori said, hugging herself. "You used to do that all the time when you were in Homicide. How the hell did you stand it? It's unbearable."

Marti lit a cigarette, took a drag, and exhaled slowly. "I didn't. I just got good at hiding it."

She watched the smoke swirl, then nodded toward the curb. "Go warm up the car. I'll be there in ten."

Then she turned, walked toward a dark sedan with blacked-out windows, and knocked on the passenger side glass.

"Hi Heather," Marti said as she sat down. She closed the door. "I was talking with the Prestons in apartment 719."

"And?" Heather asked.

Marti smiled. "And you've never heard of them, have you? I didn't think so. Look, I'm not a terrible person. We just didn't get off on the right foot. I want to fix that. I respect you." It delighted Marti that her voice sounded sincere when she said that.

"Right," Heather said.

"They are Elizabeth, Ria and William Preston. I just told them William is dead. William is Andreas Katsaros."

"What?" Heather asked. She is sticking with one-word responses, Marti thought.

"Yes. I've left a file with them. Marriage certificates, photos, the whole thing. I gave them your name. They are upset, but I said I'd speak to you. I also told them to hire a lawyer."

"Why?" Heather asked.

"Well, you wrongly arrested me, so I have good reason."

"I did not wrongly arrest you. Why do you keep saying that?" Heather protested.

Marti was relieved she got more than one word from Heather. "It really was a false arrest. I get it, I understand. I hated admitting when I arrested the wrong person too."

"That's not what happened," Heather said. She was becoming agitated, and Marti didn't want that.

"Okay. Listen, how about this? Go talk to the Prestons and if you think I am being on the up-and-up and helpful, then call me. Thank me. Take me out for a drink. If I'm not being helpful, arrest me for obstruction. Deal?" Marti asked.

Heather stared hard at Marti before finally agreeing. "And don't think I won't arrest you," Heather said.

"I wouldn't have told you if I wasn't sure. I drink whiskey, so we have to go to an actual bar," Marti said as she exited the car. As Marti walked to her own car, she heard Heather get out of hers.

"What did you two talk about?" Lori asked.

Marti started the engine. "I told her about the Prestons and said she had to take me out for a drink as a thank you. Plus, if she is busy here, I can get my inhalers inside without worrying about her seeing me. Hope you're rested, because my car needs a wash."

"You are something else," Lori said. "I'm almost impressed."

Chapter 19

Marti and Lori had just confirmed that Heather knew nothing about Andreas's second family. It was a big help to Heather, and that meant Marti won the bet.

Marti dropped Lori off at the office before heading to her apartment to take care of a few things.

They needed to talk to Henrick and Isabella, to tell them about the second family, and ask them to pass on Marti's contact information to friends and business associates so they could get in touch. She wondered if she should contact the other big players in the Falls City drug scene, but decided not to.

Marti went to light a cigarette and realized she needed to buy more. Marti turned down an alley and parked her car just a few feet in, blocking the lane but shortening her walk to the front of the bodega.

"Hey Carlos! How's it going, man?" she asked as she bounced into her local store. "Did I thank you for that orange the other day? Thanks. It was so nice," Marti said.

"You're welcome Marti. What can I get you today?" Carlos asked. He rarely looked at Marti when she was in. He was always scanning the mirrors in the store to watch his sketchy customers. Today, he had his eye on a young dude who looked around way too much. The kid walked out, but Carlos kept looking.

"A carton of smokes and a couple of bottles," Marti said. Distractedly, Carlos retrieved Marti's favorite cigarettes and whiskey. "What are you looking at?"

"That's $235. I'm looking at a guy who just pulled up and is looking in the store. Really looking. Someone following you?"

Marti laughed. "Probably. Black car?" she said, tapping her credit to pay for her purchase.

"No," Carlos said, shaking his head. "Dirty white car. Older model. Hateful looking guy," he said. "You be careful."

"I think it's the Feds. They're harmless assholes. But I'll be careful. Can I use your back door?"

"Yeah, yeah, of course," Carlos said as he waved his hand.

Marti took a quick look at the car before heading out the back door. She drove down the alley and rounded the corner, hoping to catch up with whoever was following her. She was out of luck. Marti gave Carlos a nod as she drove past.

The drive to her apartment was a little twistier than normal, but Marti had to be certain no one was following her. She parked, grabbed her cigarettes, whiskey, and Shadow, and walked up five flights of stairs.

Marti's hands moved with efficiency, her movements guided by the familiar routine of hiding her vices. She slipped one inhaler into her sock, the cool metal a familiar comfort against her skin. She carefully stashed away the remaining inhalers, their presence concealed from prying eyes.

She reached for the two bottles of whiskey. One bottle found its place on the shelf. However, she had a different purpose in mind for the other bottle. Marti's hoodie pocket, a secret repository of her hidden indulgences, welcomed the bottle.

Leaving the mess behind, she left, her footsteps echoing in the quiet apartment. Her destination: the office. The windshield wipers were working overtime. The drive went fast, and no one followed her.

Marti headed to the office with an inhaler in her sock, the bottle in her hoodie, and a cigarette between her lips. She sprinted into the office building to avoid a good soaking. When she arrived, Henrick and Isabella were waiting.

"Thanks for coming. Let's go into my office," Marti said, ushering them in. She waved Lori in and mouthed, "record this." The windows echoed with the rhythmic tapping of raindrops. Bertha sat, staring in.

"I know this is hard for you. And I'm sorry to say, I'm going to make it worse," Marti said, lighting up a cigarette. A stream of smoke escaped through her nose as she exhaled.

"Why do you hate me?" Isabella cried out. Henrick reached out to hug his mother and simultaneously shot Marti an angry look. Lori looked quizzically at Marti, but all Marti could do was shrug.

"I don't hate you. I don't care about you. Now, I care about Andreas because the more I know about him, the more likely I am to find his killer," Marti said. She knew it sounded cold-hearted; she was cold-hearted.

"You're a bastard," Henrick said as he pulled his phone out of his pocket, looked at the black screen, and put it away.

"Yep."

"We aren't paying you to find his killer. That's what the police are for," Isabella protested. She reached into her purse and pulled out a small vial. Widow's little helper. Thrown back, swallowed hard. A cough, and it was going to be better soon.

"Not you. An anonymous benefactor. Your husband was well-loved and respected. They want to make sure the police do their job," Marti said.

Marti was getting a lot of underserved hate, making her next painful statement easier. "Do you know about Elizabeth and Ria Preston?" Isabella's eyes filled with concern and she shook her head.

"Who are they? Who are they?" Henrick demanded.

Marti's eyes quickly flickered to Lori before she responded. "Andreas had a complicated life. He had a second family. The Preston's were...are, his other wife and daughter."

"Other what?"

"Other family. I've got it confirmed. He was married for a long time to another woman." Marti pulled out a marriage certificate and a photo of Andreas they would never have seen before. The one Elizabeth gave her.

Marti watched as Isabella and Henrick absorbed the revelation, their faces etched with shock and disbelief.

They were much more reserved than Ria and Elizabeth had been. Almost silent.

As the initial shock subsided, questions swirled in their minds, each one a jagged fragment of a shattered illusion. How could Andreas have led two lives, seamlessly weaving two families into his existence? What secrets had he kept hidden, and what other lies had he woven into their shared tapestry of memories?

Marti offered what little information she could. They did not hire her to investigate the bigamy. In fact, they were no longer her clients at all. She listened impatiently as they poured out their feelings, their voices echoing the confusion and pain that gripped their hearts. Marti just wanted it over with.

She rose to signal an end to the conversation. "I am sure you know, a Federal agent is investigating his death. There are going to be some unpleasant truths that come out. But I'm sure the experts will do an excellent job." Marti choked on the words.

Lori kindly ushered the pair out of the office, promising to forward any outstanding information on the case. She knew there was none to give. Ari had been very specific that the family did not know about the drug connection, and they were not going to tell them.

"They handled that better than the Prestons," Marti said after they had left the office.

Lori shook her head. "What are you thinking?"

"I'm thinking they had resources to kill him. They find out about the Prestons. Then they hire me to 'find' Andreas just in time for him to be killed. It casts suspicion on the Prestons while making the Katsaros clan look concerned and innocent. At least to a dumb Fed."

Marti clapped her hands, startling Lori. "Right. Next stop, coroner's office," she said gleefully.

"And Ha-Yoon?"

"Of course. I need a good fuck."

Chapter 20

Ha-Yoon was on the phone when Marti arrived and two other people stood waiting to speak with her. Marti took a seat in a row of blue fabric chairs and waited. Ha-Yoon wrapped up her conversation in Korean, Marti presumed, and turned her attention to the first person waiting.

The guy asked for information on how to claim a body. She gave him paperwork and a website address. The second person asked how to claim a dead person's property. Ha-Yoon directed her to the local police station. It was Marti's turn.

"I'd like information on Andreas Katsaros. Came in–" Marti began.

"I know him. He's a popular guy. Let me retrieve the file," Ha-Yoon said as she turned her attention to the computer.

Marti frowned and lit a cigarette. "Popular how?"

"Is it still raining?" Ha-Yoon asked. She did not turn away from her screen.

"Always raining. Yes. Have people been asking about him?"

"Katsaros. Yes. Federal agent Heather Blair, son Henrick Katsaros. They signed in. An unidentified man refused to sign in, so I denied him access," Ha-Yoon said. "Can I register your visit?"

"Yeah. I've been hired to find out what happened to him. What can you tell me?" Marti asked.

"What can you give me?" Ha-Yoon asked, looking up at Marti with a smile. "And don't you tell me it's hugs and kisses. Ha! My husband called. He wants a night of hugs, kisses, snuggles and back rubs. Boring!"

Marti laughed. "I'd never snuggle with you," she said with a grin.

"Good. We can use my car by the dumpsters. First, what do you want on Katsaros?"

"Everything."

Ha-Yoon turned back to the computer. "Andreas Katsaros. Fifty-one, 5 foot 10 inches tall. Single stab wound to the chest. Hit the heart, died instantly. That's all they have so far," Ha-Yoon said.

"Personal property?"

Ha-Yoon tapped and clicked and pulled up a list of personal property found on and near the victim. "Well, he was quite the adventurer. Leather jacket, cock ring, butt plug. Leather face mask. That's it."

"Shit. Do you have a photo of the jacket?" Marti said, leaning over Ha-Yoon's desk to look. Ha-Yoon clicked a few times, and an image appeared on the screen.

"Damn Marti, is that your jacket?" Ha-Yoon asked as she jabbed the screen.

"Zoom in. Shit. Looks like he was wearing the jacket when he died. Look at that blood. And Heather said I might get it back. Liar."

"Marti! My DNA is all over that damn jacket! What happened?" Ha-Yoon hissed.

"That is what I am trying to figure out. Don't worry, there's a lot of DNA on that jacket. The cops know it was mine. They have my DNA on file from when I was a cop. Do they have yours?" Marti asked.

Ha-Yoon shook her head. "No. But what if they trace me? Think I am the killer?"

Marti laughed. "Your DNA is vaginal and oral secretions. Not even the Feds are stupid enough to think you stabbed him using your cunt. Don't worry, they won't tie you to it. Don't worry."

"Don't worry. Don't worry. I'm going to worry." Ha-Yoon pushed back from her desk and glared hard. "Are you going to steal the jacket back?"

"I can't do that, Ha-Yoon," Marti said as she shook her head. "It's one thing when it's a low profile case. But this one..."

"High profile? Why?"

Marti tapped her fingers on the desk while she studied the woodgrain. "Look, I've been hired to find out who killed him. I'll find him. You'll be fine," she said. She was fairly certain that was all true.

Ha-Yoon rolled forward inch by inch until she was pressed against her side of the desk.

"You owe me big," Ha-Yoon said.

"Anything you want," Marti said. "Anything." She smiled and licked her lips.

Ha-Yoon's eyes sparkled as she pulled travel-sized lube from her purse. She pressed them into Marti's hand. "Change of plans," she said, voice hot with promise. "Out back. My silver car. Ten minutes."

Marti's mouth curled into a wicked grin as she tucked the lube into her hoodie pocket.

Outside, rain slicked the pavement in reflective streaks under weak security lights. Marti smoked her cigarette behind a dumpster, waiting until Ha-Yoon finally emerged into the downpour like a woman walking into her own undoing.

She slammed the car door shut behind her. The passenger door creaked open half a second later, and Ha-Yoon stepped in. Composed as always, her dark blouse immaculate even after twelve hours sitting at a sterile computer desk. Her presence stole the air.

"You ready?" she asked without looking at Marti.

Marti didn't answer. She was already crawling over the center console like a woman possessed, mouth hungry for skin she'd memorized.

Ha-Yoon tilted her head back against the seat rest with a sigh that wasn't quite boredom. More like indulgent expectation.

The car filled with the soft whisper of shifting fabric as Marti pushed up Ha-Yoon's skirt. Her hands trembled only slightly as she framed those thighsale, smooth despite her age, strong and ready.

"You wore lace today." Marti's voice was reverent. "You knew."

"I always know," Ha-Yoon murmured without smiling.

She lifted her hips lazily, allowing Marti to strip her panties down: black chiffon edged in embroidery so delicate it caught on Marti's finger. The intimacy of this ritual never dulled. Every time felt like a ceremony, a temple visit where Ha-Yoon was goddess and altar both.

Marti held the panties up to her face for a moment, just enough to inhale once, and then shoved them down her own jeans with precision. The silk was already warm against her labia, sticky with anticipation before she had even made contact with Ha-Yoon's cunt.

She didn't ask permission to slide between Ha-Yoon's legs; she never needed to. This was understood: access granted not through affection but obsession. Service. Worship.

Ha-Yoon shifted slightly in her seat, pressing one heel against the dash, opening wider: her only signal that she expected expert attention now and not later.

Marti kissed first: slow drags of tongue along inner thigh, inhaling sweat and office air conditioning. Then she moaned involuntarily as her lips met slick heat. Ha-Yoon was already wet.

Good girl, Marti thought silently about herself. Like a dog.

The smell sharpened as she pressed deeper, tongue flattening against labia first before finding rhythm: steady swirls around swollen clit while her hand slid shamelessly down into her own jeans. The panties stuck to everything inside; they were soaked now from both of them.

Ha-Yoon exhaled above, voice low but dominant: "Don't stop this time."

Marti whimpered into her cunt in response. Over-stimulation from trying to match two pleasures at once: tongue working deeper while fingers inside her own pants rubbed against lace-wrapped folds.

Outside the windshield: rain.

Inside this car: slick sounds of service-masturbation symphony. One woman stretched open but untouched by anything except breath and tongue; another moaning qui-etly into surrender with panties clenched between trem-bling fingers.

Ha-Yoon didn't come loudly, she never did, just arched slightly when it hit and uttered one syllable like punctua-tion: "Yes." Cold and sharp like scalpel steel.

Marti kept licking even after. Past orgasm into after-shock territory where sensitivity borders on pain, because stopping felt wrong until she was told otherwise.

Eventually, nails tapped gently on Marti's scalp; not af-fectionate exactly, more dismissal than caress. Still sacred.

Marti pulled back slowly. Her face was slick with Ha-Yoon's release; mouth red and raw from effort. She sat back in her seat without speaking, still breathing fast from fingering herself to climax during worship. Her hand came out sticky and damp. She licked it clean without shame.

"That was...decent," Ha-Yoon finally said, adjusting her skirt again as if nothing had happened at all.

Marti smiled faintly. She could still feel those panties stuck damply against her groin like a promise of future pleasure. "I'm keeping your panties, they're mine to play with."

Fucking Ha-Yoon in the parking lot had been exhausting. She had no idea how a woman so close to retirement had such a powerful sex drive, but it was something Marti aspired to.

Chapter 21

Sleep after wild sex was almost always fantastic, and Marti woke feeling refreshed. After a shower, she drove to work, almost happy until she passed a burned-out building with fresh graffiti. 29-9 in bleeding red paint.

She slowed, recognizing the Zenzar's charred facade. One of Ari Stirling's clubs. Someone had sent him a message he wouldn't miss.

That was a 'him' problem. The fucking traffic was a 'her' problem, and Marti's horn took the brunt of her anger for the entire seven-minute drive to the office.

The offices for Martina Starova Investigations had no bookcases groaning under the weight of leather bound law books. No spinning globes. No awards of merit. It was personable, unthreatening.

The only view out the window was a fire escape that occasionally held a cat. The worn leather couch was for sex and sleeping, not for guests to sit. And yet there she was. Ria Preston was sitting on the couch, crying. It did not make Marti happy.

Lori deliberately stood in the doorway, arms crossed, watching. Judging. Marti lit a cigarette and waited for at least some tears to subside.

"I'm sorry Ria. I'm sorry your mother was arrested. But I have nothing to do with it," Marti said. She was getting saltier by the minute. With the arrest of Elizabeth Preston for the murder of her husband, Marti might have to return most of Ari's fee.

She blew smoke rings and thought. "Look, let me try talking to the Feds. Maybe I can get something from them," Marti offered. "But honestly, from an objective point of view, your mother is a strong suspect. The wronged wife who lived in poverty while another family lived in luxury? It's a textbook reason for murder," Marti said.

"But we didn't know about the other family," Ria said between sobs.

"You didn't know about the other family. We don't know what your mother knew. Did you tell your mother you hired a private investigator to find your dad?" Marti asked.

"Yes, she's the one who gave me the $100," Ria said.

Marti scratched her head and stubbed her cigarette out. "Your mother gave you $100 and told you to hire a private investigator. It sounds like she was trying to find him, track him down. You hire me, I find him, he dies. It doesn't look good."

"But we didn't know," Ria protested. Lori handed her another tissue and set a small trash can near her.

"I saw him just before he died. If she followed me, she would have known where he was," Marti said.

Ria set her jaw and stood up. "How dare you say my mother killed my father!" Her face turned red and the tears in her eyes replaced with fire.

Marti stood up to walk Ria out. As she approached, Ria lashed out and slapped Marti across the face. Instinctively, Marti's hand balled up in a fist, ready to hit back. Lori grabbed Ria by the shoulders to usher her out. "Always the face," Marti laughed. Lori locked the door after Ria and returned to Marti.

"You okay there, Mother Teresa?" she asked, her eyes full of mirth.

"That was just a love tap. Reminds me of my last relationship. But without the scar tissue," Marti joked. She was thinking of Pauline's drug-induced attack that left her bruised and battered.

"What do you think of the arrest?" Lori asked.

Marti reached for the bottle of whiskey in her desk drawer and pulled out two glasses. Lori always turned it down, but Marti thought it important to offer. Lori shook her head and Marti poured herself a shot. She sat on the couch, took a sip, and put the glass down on the table beside her.

"It only makes sense if Heather has evidence I don't know about."

"You said you needed her on your side to get access to information."

"Okay, remind me. What are the red flags for Elizabeth? Look up the file, won't you?"

"Yep. My office," Lori said as she retreated to her desk. Marti followed and sat down. She put her feet up on the other chair.

"Okay," Lori said as she opened up files and reports. "Elizabeth Preston. Andreas divorced her last year and moved out. He maintained a separate apartment, which says something."

"What does it say?"

"I have no idea. You're the expert," Lori laughed.

"Okay, yeah. It says a couple of things. One is, he wanted to maintain the façade of the family. He could have just disappeared, but he stayed accessible. Do we have the divorce papers? Do we know if Elizabeth saw Andreas after the divorce? Like, keep a sexual relationship going? Is that why he wanted an apartment?"

Lori looked through her files, focussing on financials. "Not that we know of, but who knows? I don't have the divorce papers. But I know that Elizabeth had a gambling problem. She had no income other than Andreas's fake job income. That was pretty sparse. And Elizabeth gambled at the local casinos. It's on her credit card statements. Not massive amounts, not enough to lose the house. But enough to…To make Andreas want to divorce her to avoid being sucked into a bankruptcy. That would have exposed him."

"That's a motive for him to kill her, not the other way around. What about Ria? She knew about the apartment."

"Both she and her mother knew."

"Nah. If it was either of them, I think they'd have gone to the apartment. Some place he was familiar with, they were all familiar with. A place to catch him off guard."

"So, no?"

Marti nodded and lit a cigarette. "I'm not feeling it. Not Elizabeth. She seemed truly distraught when we told her."

"If her daughter has her temper…"

"Being betrayed half your life can turn a woman bitter."

"Can you work the Heather angle? Get information?"

"I'm going to have to. She solved the case for us," Marti said with a grin.

Lori's eyes narrowed. "Why are you smiling just because she arrested someone? We'll lose the money from Ari," Lori said.

Marti took a deep drag and blew the smoke out loudly. "It may not look like it, but it means Heather helped us with our investigation."

Lori's eyes widened. "Oh no, no, no. That's not the bet."

"That's exactly the bet." Marti stood up. "If Heather 'substantively helps with our investigation,' and I'd say arresting someone substantively helps. You lost."

"Damn it! I was so sure," Lori said.

Marti looked at the time. "Look at that. Lots of time, let's go."

"Oh, no."

"You can't back out when you lose."

"Marti, it's raining. I'll get a cold. My clothes will get soaked."

"If only you knew what I did last night in the rain. But that's a whole other thing. This is washing my car in your underwear. Your clothes can stay here," Marti offered.

"We don't have car soap."

"Car soap? No. Nothing called car soap. Just means you will have to rub harder."

Lori crossed her arms and pouted. "Fine. Move the car around back. And no masturbating. No! Don't give me that look. That wasn't part of the deal."

Marti nodded and dug an inhaler out of her desk drawer and stuck it in her pocket. "Out back. In five," Marti said, and left. Her heart was racing as she headed downstairs. She'd already imagined Lori stripping for her. This car wash was going to be fantasy fodder for a while.

Chapter 22

Sleep after wild sex was almost always fantastic, and Marti woke feeling refreshed. After a shower, she drove to work, almost happy until she passed a burned-out building with fresh graffiti. 29-9 in bleeding red paint.

She slowed, recognizing the Zenzar's charred facade. One of Ari Stirling's clubs. Someone had sent him a message he wouldn't miss.

That was a 'him' problem. The fucking traffic was a 'her' problem, and Marti's horn took the brunt of her anger for the entire seven-minute drive to the office.

The offices for Martina Starova Investigations had no bookcases groaning under the weight of leather bound law books. No spinning globes. No awards of merit. It was personable, unthreatening.

The only view out the window was a fire escape that occasionally held a cat. The worn leather couch was for sex and sleeping, not for guests to sit. And yet there she was. Ria Preston was sitting on the couch, crying. It did not make Marti happy.

Lori deliberately stood in the doorway, arms crossed, watching. Judging. Marti lit a cigarette and waited for at least some tears to subside.

"I'm sorry Ria. I'm sorry your mother was arrested. But I have nothing to do with it," Marti said. She was getting saltier by the minute. With the arrest of Elizabeth Preston for the murder of her husband, Marti might have to return most of Ari's fee.

She blew smoke rings and thought. "Look, let me try talking to the Feds. Maybe I can get something from them," Marti offered. "But honestly, from an objective point of view, your mother is a strong suspect. The wronged wife who lived in poverty while another family lived in luxury? It's a textbook reason for murder," Marti said.

"But we didn't know about the other family," Ria said between sobs.

"You didn't know about the other family. We don't know what your mother knew. Did you tell your mother you hired a private investigator to find your dad?" Marti asked.

"Yes, she's the one who gave me the $100," Ria said.

Marti scratched her head and stubbed her cigarette out. "Your mother gave you $100 and told you to hire a private investigator. It sounds like she was trying to find him, track him down. You hire me, I find him, he dies. It doesn't look good."

"But we didn't know," Ria protested. Lori handed her another tissue and set a small trash can near her.

"I saw him just before he died. If she followed me, she would have known where he was," Marti said.

Ria set her jaw and stood up. "How dare you say my mother killed my father!" Her face turned red and the tears in her eyes replaced with fire.

Marti stood up to walk Ria out. As she approached, Ria lashed out and slapped Marti across the face. Instinctively, Marti's hand balled up in a fist, ready to hit back. Lori grabbed Ria by the shoulders to usher her out. "Always the face," Marti laughed. Lori locked the door after Ria and returned to Marti.

"You okay there, Mother Teresa?" she asked, her eyes full of mirth.

"That was just a love tap. Reminds me of my last relationship. But without the scar tissue," Marti joked. She was thinking of Pauline's drug-induced attack that left her bruised and battered.

"What do you think of the arrest?" Lori asked.

Marti reached for the bottle of whiskey in her desk drawer and pulled out two glasses. Lori always turned it down, but Marti thought it important to offer. Lori shook her head and Marti poured herself a shot. She sat on the couch, took a sip, and put the glass down on the table beside her.

"It only makes sense if Heather has evidence I don't know about."

"You said you needed her on your side to get access to information."

"Okay, remind me. What are the red flags for Elizabeth? Look up the file, won't you?"

"Yep. My office," Lori said as she retreated to her desk. Marti followed and sat down. She put her feet up on the other chair.

"Okay," Lori said as she opened up files and reports. "Elizabeth Preston. Andreas divorced her last year and moved out. He maintained a separate apartment, which says something."

"What does it say?"

"I have no idea. You're the expert," Lori laughed.

"Okay, yeah. It says a couple of things. One is, he wanted to maintain the façade of the family. He could have just disappeared, but he stayed accessible. Do we have the divorce papers? Do we know if Elizabeth saw Andreas after the divorce? Like, keep a sexual relationship going? Is that why he wanted an apartment?"

Lori looked through her files, focussing on financials. "Not that we know of, but who knows? I don't have the divorce papers. But I know that Elizabeth had a gambling problem. She had no income other than Andreas's fake job income. That was pretty sparse. And Elizabeth gambled at the local casinos. It's on her credit card statements. Not massive amounts, not enough to lose the house. But enough to…To make Andreas want to divorce her to avoid being sucked into a bankruptcy. That would have exposed him."

"That's a motive for him to kill her, not the other way around. What about Ria? She knew about the apartment."

"Both she and her mother knew."

"Nah. If it was either of them, I think they'd have gone to the apartment. Some place he was familiar with, they were all familiar with. A place to catch him off guard."

"So, no?"

Marti nodded and lit a cigarette. "I'm not feeling it. Not Elizabeth. She seemed truly distraught when we told her."

"If her daughter has her temper…"

"Being betrayed half your life can turn a woman bitter."

"Can you work the Heather angle? Get information?"

"I'm going to have to. She solved the case for us," Marti said with a grin.

Lori's eyes narrowed. "Why are you smiling just because she arrested someone? We'll lose the money from Ari," Lori said.

Marti took a deep drag and blew the smoke out loudly. "It may not look like it, but it means Heather helped us with our investigation."

Lori's eyes widened. "Oh no, no, no. That's not the bet."

"That's exactly the bet." Marti stood up. "If Heather 'substantively helps with our investigation,' and I'd say arresting someone substantively helps. You lost."

"Damn it! I was so sure," Lori said.

Marti looked at the time. "Look at that. Lots of time, let's go."

"Oh, no."

"You can't back out when you lose."

"Marti, it's raining. I'll get a cold. My clothes will get soaked."

"If only you knew what I did last night in the rain. But that's a whole other thing. This is washing my car in your underwear. Your clothes can stay here," Marti offered.

"We don't have car soap."

"Car soap? No. Nothing called car soap. Just means you will have to rub harder."

Lori crossed her arms and pouted. "Fine. Move the car around back. And no masturbating. No! Don't give me that look. That wasn't part of the deal."

Marti nodded and dug an inhaler out of her desk drawer and stuck it in her pocket. "Out back. In five," Marti said, and left. Her heart was racing as she headed downstairs. She'd already imagined Lori stripping for her. This car wash was going to be fantasy fodder for a while.

Chapter 23

After her conversation with Heather about Elizabeth Preston's arrest, Marti headed to her next appointment for the day.

She drove an hour and a half to New Dutch City, just to stand outside the offices of GenoHealth Solutions for twenty minutes, waiting for Henrick Katsaros. She leaned against the hood of her car, smoking a cigarette. Marti delighted in the dirty looks she was getting from the people walking in and out of the building.

She wondered if GenoHealth constructed the building, or if they'd bought it. Its sleek, contemporary design commanded attention, with a façade of reflective golden glass panels that stood out from the surrounding urban landscape. The company's sophisticated logo, which Marti decided was some kind of genotype infinity symbol, exuded a sense of modernity and cutting-edge innovation.

New Dutch City was an open, bright city that had not fallen into the over-building of concrete towers that darkened Falls City. From what she heard, they also managed to escape the political corruption, drugs and crime that riddled Falls City. New Dutch City was Eden compared to her hometown.

"Marti?" Henrick said, bringing her out of her revery. "Thanks for coming. This means so much to me," he said. He extended his hand. "I knew my father was well-loved. But you won't tell me who hired you to keep investigating?"

Marti shook hands. "Sorry, the person asked to remain anonymous. Thanks for arranging this." The entrance, marked by imposing doors, opened into a spacious lobby. She looked past security to the bank of elevators and could feel her heart jackhammer. Fucking elevators. Somewhere along the lines, Marti had developed claustrophobia.

Henrick and Marti walked past security, and a shimmer of perspiration formed on her brow. They walked into the lobby between the sets of elevators, and her hands shook. An elevator dinged, and Marti almost stumbled as her knees gave way.

When Henrick walked straight through the elevator lobby and turned a corner, Marti bumped inelegantly against the wall in her rush to follow him. She was grateful for small mercies as a massive marble staircase loomed in front of them.

"My father's office is on the second floor," Henrick said, as he headed up the stairs. "He hated elevators. Thought the cable would break, and he'd fall to his death."

"Silly idea," Marti laughed.

"Too many action movies. This is us," he said. A tall man nodded and opened the door for Henrick as he approached, but held his hand out to stop Marti.

"Is it not obvious she's with me? Moron!" Henrick snapped. Marti made a shocked face to let the man know she didn't share Henrick's sentiment.

"The Board has to clear everyone who walks into the office, sir," he replied. "Name please?"

"Martina Starova."

"One moment." He turned his attention to his phone while Marti waited patiently. Henrick waited less patiently, huffing loudly and pacing. The phone dinged, and the man said, "You're clear. Welcome Ms. Starova. Please see me when you leave."

Marti nodded. He was standing directly in front of the only door to the office. There was no way not to see him when she left. Marti joined Henrick in Andreas's office. It was a massive office, befitting the CEO of a multinational medical company.

"Someone's been through here, yes?" Marti asked as she looked around. There was no computer, no paper, no waste basket. The bookshelf behind the desk held only an empty yet stylish vase, a globe, and a couple of books laying on their sides. On the desk was a pen holder, three framed family photos of Andreas, Isabella, and Henrick, and two notepads. No photos of Katarina.

"The Board of Directors swooped in quickly," Henrick said. "I think they took some personal items. I gave him a Fassbinder pen, and it's missing. Mother gave him a hand-crafted leather document tray. Gone. I have no idea what they're doing with those personal items, but they won't give them back," he whined.

"Can you draw up a list for me? If you have any pho-tos of personal items, that would be helpful," Marti said. "Send it to Lori. I don't know if it will be useful, but you'll at least need it to make an insurance claim."

Henrick nodded, sat down in a chair by the window, and created a list. Marti looked at the polished marble floor and could see a dark figure in the doorway. The man at the door was watching everything she was doing, listening to everything she was saying. She expected nothing less from Ari.

Marti turned her attention to the desk. She looked in the drawers and saw nothing but paperclips and dust. It didn't matter. Marti squeezed her ear and took a photograph. In the next drawer was more dust and a stain.

Click.

Marti took photos of the penholder and each pen. She moved the notepads to see them better and settled into the lush leather chair. She turned every page and snapped a photo. There were dick doodles that could have been drawn by a 10-year-old boy. Spirals and circles that could have been drawn by a MethLumina addict. There was a grocery shopping list.

A series of certificates and diplomas were clustered on the wall. She took a photograph of each one. There were five swords hanging in another cluster, but there was an empty spot that held a sixth. Marti paused and knew she needed to find out more about Andreas's wound.

Click.

"Did your father collect swords?" Marti asked.

"Yes. Gladius, he called them. Used by ancient Roman foot soldiers. But I can't tell you much about them."

"You know what this one was?" she asked, pointing to the empty spot.

Henrick shook his head. "He stabbed his accountant with it years ago."

"His...?"

Henrick shrugged. "Dad did three months. The accountant got twenty years for fraud, and a great scar to show off in prison. Win-win." After another few seconds of glaring, Henrick returned his attention to his phone.

Marti took photos of every book after flipping through all the pages, the vase, and the globe. She took a photo of Henrick and of the man at the door.

"I've sent the list to your secretary," Henrick announced.

"Great. I have nothing else," Marti said. "Oh, what about these family photos? Do you want them?"

"Nothing leaves the office," the doorman said. Marti put them back on the desk. She and Henrick walked out, Marti giving a courteous nod to the doorman as she passed by.

As they walked back to the lobby, Marti advised Henrick that nothing seemed useful in the office but that she had various lines of inquiry. It was a lie; she had no lines of inquiry. Marti knew it was a bad idea to say that to a client. "Before I go, I'm sorry, but you know I have to check. Where were–"

"We were at dinner at Hobemme's on Tenth Avenue."

Marti made a note of the plural pronoun. It was raining as she and Henrick left the building. The next stop was the Katsaros home. Marti would follow Henrick's car. Heading to her car, Marti held out her hand and let the rain fall into her palm. She rubbed her fingers together. Even the rain seems cleaner here.

Chapter 24

Marti called Lori as she was following Henrick's car to the family home. "Hey. There was almost nothing in his office. I'll send the photos. The Board put a man on the door, which means there's something still there, but they probably haven't found it either. Find out about his swords. Gladiolas or...no Roman Gladius. Look for collectors, groups, whatever. One was missing."

"Yes, sure thing. I'll go over the notebooks. I have the list of personal items from Henrick. I'll send it back to you, so you can compare with what's at the house," Lori said. "And I've been working on getting financials, but I haven't found anything yet."

"Haven't found anything? Like, no bank accounts or credit?"

"Not yet. Ask Henrick or Isabella," Lori said.

Marti lit a cigarette. "Something isn't right. Did you look under Preston?" She rolled down the window to let the smoke escape. It was her way of making Upper Henley just a little more polluted.

"Of course I did," Lori said.

"Phone dumps?"

"Not easy, but I'm trying."

"Henrick said he was at Hobemme's on Tenth Avenue when his father died. Double-check. I'm here. Send me all that shit," Marti said before hanging up.

Lori quickly started digging in on the swords. There might be someone out there who knows something. As soon as they hung up, Lori set to work. She turned to the Internet in search of any information related to Gladius collectors or enthusiasts.

Lori scoured online forums and websites dedicated to the ancient weapons. She found the trading to be active, but everything looked legitimate. No one she could find was offering an undocumented Gladius for sale. It looked like a dead end.

Marti was at the Katsaros home, a sprawling structure, with multiple levels and expansive windows that allowed for plenty of natural light to flood into the space. Its exterior was luxurious, but not ostentatious, blending seamlessly into the boring suburban landscape it called home. This neighborhood valued money and pretending not to have it, and the Katsaros' residence embodied those ideals perfectly. Yet, beneath its unassuming facade, there was an air of sophistication and refinement that could only be found in a wealthy enclave like this one. Despite its size and grandeur, the house exuded a sense of comfort and familiarity, as if it belonged exactly where it stood. In this community, being average was a virtue, and the Katsaros family fit right in.

Drug money in the 'burbs.

Marti parked the car with a gentle purr and clicked off the engine. She stepped out, her boots sinking into the soft gravel driveway. Henrick joined her and together they approached the unlocked home, the front door creaking open with a faint groan. Inside, the house was quiet and still, as if holding its breath in anticipation of their arrival. They had painted the walls a bland beige, lacking any personality or character. There were no photos or decorations on display, leaving it feeling empty and devoid of life. It seemed unworthy of attention, just another mundane structure blending into the surrounding neighborhood. Marti took photos anyway.

"Drink? FrostFire Vodka," Henrick said as he reached into a cabinet. He was offering the cheapest bottle he had.

"Yeah, please," Marti said.

"Hell no," Isabella said, walking into the living room. "You're here to snoop on my husband's private life. Just get it over with." Her tone was as flat as the color scheme.

"Of course. Henrick, can you show me around?" Marti asked. The sooner she could leave this yawn-inducing hell, the better. It took Marti three minutes to walk through the bedroom. Permeating the room was the smell of laundry soap, probably named something like Cotton Candy Honeydew Cloud Burst. There was nothing at all of the couple she'd met at the sex club. Not the smell of sex, not the smell of bleach to remove the smell of sex. There were no holes in the ceiling showing a swing had been removed, no jizz stains on the floor.

There were also no family photos, no bedside lamps, no extra pillows on the bed. Andreas and Isabella did not use this room, ever. It was a ploy.

"Did your father have a home office?" she asked.

Henrick led her to a small room with a laptop, a desk, and a dictionary. "Before you ask, I don't have the password for the laptop," Henrick offered.

Marti nodded. "Can I take it? In case my secretary can do something with it."

"Mom? Can Marti have dad's laptop?"

"You don't have to yell. I'm right here," Isabella said as she walked into the room. "Honey, give us a minute, would you?"

Henrick walked out and Isabella shut the door after him. She turned and looked Marti up and down. "I really wanted you to fuck me," Isabella said. She pushed herself off the door and sat in the office chair. "But somehow, I ended up a widow instead." The words rang out sharply, like a whip cracking in the air. "If you'd only obeyed orders, my husband might still be alive."

Isabella's voice was cold and accusatory. Marti remained silent, steeling herself for the tirade of blame that would follow. She could feel her heart racing, but Isabella held her scathing lecture. Where were the words of anguish and blame?

"I thought he was you for a minute. He was wearing a mask, and he had your jacket on. I could smell you. I thought it was you until he got close to my face, and then I smelled his breath. His breath always smells like popcorn... Smelled. Like popcorn."

"I..."

Isabella's voice trembled as she spoke, her eyes brimming with unshed tears. "I know you're sorry. It wasn't your fault. I'm not trying to blame you. I really loved my husband."

She stood up and reached for the laptop, clutching it tightly to her chest. Slowly, she made her way over to Marti and placed the laptop in her hands. "The password is 'password'," she whispered, her voice cracking with emotion. Her voice trailed off as she fought back a sob, unable to finish her sentence. "Please," she implored, her eyes begging Marti to fulfill her request. "Find out who killed him."

Chapter 25

The drive from bucolic Upper Henley to the foul streets of Falls City was long, and Marti was getting bored. She fiddled with the radio. But out here, in the middle of nowhere, there was nothing but talk radio. The monotonous hum of the car engine and the rhythmic swaying of the trees outside brought no excitement to her journey.

Marti glanced at the clock on the dashboard. It was already late afternoon, and the sun began its descent, casting long shadows across the desolate landscape.

Frustrated, she reached for her pack of cigarettes and pulled one out, placing it between her lips. She flicked open the car's ashtray and reached for the lighter when a sudden movement caught her eye.

In the rearview mirror, Marti could see a pair of head-lights rapidly approaching from behind. The car was gaining on her, its engine roaring like a wild beast. A surge of adrenaline shot through her veins as she realized she was being chased.

Her heart pounding, Marti pressed harder on the gas pedal, urging her wreck to go faster. But it was no match for the sleek sports car behind her. The distance between them closed rapidly, and panic gripped her chest like a vise.

As the pursuing vehicle drew alongside her, Marti caught a glimpse of the driver, a man with a scarred face and a sinister grin plastered across his lips. She could hear his deranged laughter over the roar of their engines. She pulled out her gun.

Gripping the steering wheel with one hand and firing wildly out the window with the other, Marti glanced at the road ahead. It shimmered and floated away, leaving an ocean of sand.

Marti slammed on her brakes. "What the fuck? Fucking Shadow!" Taking a deep breath to steady her nerves, Marti realized there was no other car, no scarred man, no sand. But she had let off a half dozen shots. "I gotta get off this shit." She was hallucinating even when she wasn't high, and that meant she was crossing a threshold that every

Shadow junkie knew. Once those hallucinations got hold, there was no coming back.

Marti shook her head and steadied her nerves. She put the gun back in the holster and continued her drive. Something has to give.

At the office, Marti put the laptop on Lori's desk with a thunk. "Andreas's laptop from home. Password is 'password'."

Lori looked at it and shook her head. "Really? What's on it?"

"How the fuck would I know? You're the computer expert," Marti said as she flopped into the chair and lit a cigarette.

"Yeah, it really takes an expert to know how to use a password." Lori started the computer and entered the password. The background image was Isabella, nude. "You didn't check this out?"

"Nope. Here are the earrings," Marti said as she handed over the camera equipment. She told Lori about the office and the house and her interactions with Isabella and Henrick.

"Before you get to the laptop, can you save the images on the server? I want to take another look at that notebook," Marti said as she headed to her office. "Update me in an hour."

Marti closed the door, put out her cigarette, laid down on the couch, and took a hit of Shadow. She knew it was killing her. Marti looked at the inhaler and wondered if it was worth the money anymore. She might have to find a new drug.

Twenty minutes later, Marti was already at her desk, going through the notebook. Everything was still a little fuzzy, but she liked to work that way sometimes. She looked at the photographs of the pages. Doodles. Not much more than scribbles and dicks. A few numbers that made no sense to her. '1.97+2.83 #95%'. It could be a password to something, but right now, she had no idea what it would be for. She grabbed a screen pen and circled the equation. The screen pen allowed Marti to press against the monitor and overlay the image with digital ink.

Marti highlighted an area of rage doodle–where the pen had gone over and over the same area so much it tore a hole in the paper–and adjusted the contrast. She could see no words under the mad ink.

Bertha appeared suddenly on the desk, startling Marti. "Get the fuck out," she growled. Bertha turned around to show off her tail, resulting in a swat from Marti. "I don't know why you don't speak English," she complained. "I thought cats were supposed to be smart. You should know a few languages."

Marti went to the next page, and the next. This one was full of dicks. Some with hairy balls, some ejaculating. One with an eye instead of a head. "Hey Bertha, what do you make of this?" she asked, tapping the eye. "He was a kinky guy. Think he had a thing for... eye sex? Is that a thing?" Bertha didn't answer.

Marti counted fourteen dicks on the page, and used the screen pen to make a notation, '14.'

She stared at the page for a moment longer and saw it. Taking the screen pen, she traced the ejaculate from one penis. It was just a doodle. She cleared the drawing and tried again. On the third try, Marti figured it out. "Fuck yeah!" she shouted, startling Bertha. She laughed. "Gotcha back, bitch." Marti saved the notation and went to speak with Lori.

"Akello," Marti said as she walked behind Lori's desk.

"Akello?"

"Yeah, call up the notebook. The last image edited. There! It says Akello," Marti said. She was leaning over Lori trying very hard to look at the stupid ink dick on the screen and not down Lori's top.

Lori tilted her head. "What's Akello?"

"Tomas Akello. He's a private investigator. Ha! Get it? Private investigator? Private dick?" Marti tapped the penis on the monitor to emphasize the connection.

"So Andreas drew a bunch of penises to code the last name of a private detective in ejaculate?" Lori asked.

Marti sat down opposite the desk. "You know, when you say it like that, it doesn't sound that normal. But yes, I think that's what Andreas did. I'm sure he thought it was funny. I know Tomas. Well, I know of him. He's over on Laird and Fortieth, I think. Handles divorce cases only."

"Ah, so maybe Andreas was getting a divorce?"

Marti shrugged. "Or the Preston divorce. Do we have any financials? Any payouts to a divorce lawyer?"

Lori held up her finger. "Before we go there, it seems there's more to this laptop than we were told. Check this out," she said as she spun it around for Marti to see.

Marti blinked. It was a computer screen with a few icons on it. "What am I looking at?"

"Huh?" Lori said as she spun the laptop back toward her. "Oops. Sorry, here, check this out."

Now the screen had a ledger on it. "Andreas kept all of GenoHealth's financials on his home laptop."

"Isabella gave us this?" Marti asked. She was shocked.

"Nope. Isabella gave us the way to access the shared account on the laptop. Boring stuff like emails and a few dirty pictures. No! You can look at them later," Lori said, preempting Marti's request.

"I found another account on the laptop. Andreas was not good with passwords. This administrator account had a password of '123456'."

"Maybe someone killed him for being stupid," Marti said as she lit another cigarette.

"The records for him personally are interesting, if they're accurate. It looks like everything is owned by GenoHealth, which is why we couldn't find anything under his name. This ledger, called 'Personal', lists three luxury cars, a house in Italy and another house in Mexico which appear to have been purchased by GenoHealth," Lori said. She reached over to grab the paper file on Andreas. "I'm sure he treated these things as personal assets. His cars, his homes."

"Does he own the family home?"

"Yes. But that seems to be it. Now, the assets of Geno-Health seem solid enough at first glance. But these real estate transactions, which you wouldn't expect from a medical company, you can put them together to tell a story," Lori said.

"Tell me a story," Marti said, settling in. She sucked more smoke into her lungs.

Chapter 26

Going over the financials they found on Andreas's laptop, Lori was intrigued. "GenoHealth owns thirty casinos across the US and Mexico."

Marti laughed. "Casinos? For a medical company? Is this company legit at all? I mean, any right thinking Board member is going to question that purchase."

"Didn't you say the accountant was caught defrauding the company?"

Marti paused. Tapped her finger. "So he-—"

"Or she."

"They. Bought all this shit and the company kept it after discovering the fraud?"

Lori shrugged. "If they were profitable, why not? The money was already spent. The Board probably figured they might as well keep the revenue streams. Plus, think about it: casinos are perfect money laundering operations. Cash businesses with high volume transactions."

"Jesus," Marti whispered. "So they discovered their accountant's scheme and instead of unwinding it..."

"They saw an opportunity. Medical research is expensive and unpredictable. Gambling, on the other hand..." Lori raised her eyebrows meaningfully. "The house always wins."

"Ah. Well, I can't actually prove any of it, but we don't have to. Not for what we're doing. I had the credit company send over some paper copies. It's the best they could do," she said. She pulled out some dark brown paper and handed it to Marti.

They listed the transactions in dark red ink, barely discernable by the human eye. "This is some old school shit," Marti said as she angled the paper into the light. It was shiny.

"Yes. They used a reflective paper as well, so if you take a photo or photocopy, all you get is the light reflected back. It is old school, but it hasn't been thwarted yet," Lori said. "So be careful. It's an original."

"It's not like I set stuff on fire, you know."

"You did two months ago when you fell asleep with a lit match in your hand. I don't even know how that's possible and yet, you managed it."

Marti huffed. "I was sick. I didn't fall asleep, I passed out. Different. Anyway, here, take the paper back. Does it tell us anything?"

Outside, the rain let up. Bertha meowed from Marti's office and left the duo. "You know, I wonder if that cat is a spy. Maybe has a microchip or something," Marti said.

Lori put the paper safely away. "Drugs are addling your brain."

Marti looked at her and wondered if it was Lori who had the spy microchip.

"The transactions are minor purchases. A loaf of bread, a tank of gas. Nothing to suggest he was seeing someone."

"Except for his other wife," Marti replied. "Any transactions under Preston?"

"Yes, actually. All the normal transactions and banking you'd expect to see. Except no traceable paycheck. Cash deposits every week."

"Maybe a way to fake his job?"

"Likely. Mrs. Preston gave all the information to me. It seems really simple. No house, no car. Steady income in a small weekly installment, average expenses. Nothing elaborate, no red flags. Andreas was fantastic at hiding who he was," Lori said. She leaned back in her chair and put her hands behind her head to stretch her arms out. Marti liked the view.

"I'm going to talk to Tomas Akello," Marti said, getting up. "It's possible Isabella hired him and Andreas found out."

"Would Akello kill Andreas? For money? Or love?" Lori asked.

Marti scoffed. "No. Akello is underhanded, and he's not above sleeping with his clients. But he doesn't kill for them. Although he might know a guy who knows a guy. I'll see what I can find out. Keep working on the file."

"Oh, and here I was thinking I'd just spend the afternoon doing my nails," Lori snipped.

Marti smirked and winked at Lori before heading out the door. She knew that speaking with Akello was likely to get nowhere, but she had to try. If Andreas and Isabella were divorcing, Isabella had little to gain. Andreas had no money of his own, and his business wasn't his business. It was Ari's, but Isabella didn't know that.

Marti drove past Akello's business three times. Her back ached, and she was in no mood for bullshit. She spotted a car pulling out of a nearby parking spot, and someone waiting to take it. The other driver took a split second too long, and Marti pulled into the spot.

Horns honked and cars inched past.

She smiled at the other driver, who got out of his car to scream at her. When she exited her car, he went for her. "You bastard!" he screamed.

"That's bitch to you," Marti laughed. He lunged at her, and Marti met him with a side kick to the stomach. It stopped him like a brick wall and he puked. She had to scramble quickly out of the way.

"You...you..." he gasped.

"Shut up asshole," Marti said.

"I'm calling the police!" he gasped.

"I'm calling the police," Marti whined, mocking him. "You're being mean to me. You took my parking, wah!"

More horns honked, and someone yelled at the pair.

The man spit the last of the vomit out of his mouth and squared up as if he was a prizefighter in a movie. Marti pulled her gun, and he backed up. Almost into traffic. "I don't know who you are," he growled as he wiped foam from his mouth, "But I'm going to get you back."

"Call the cops, little man," Marti snapped as she walked away. More horns honked and someone yelled at the man to move his car as he had stopped in the street.

Marti lit a cigarette and walked down the block to Akello's office. She didn't hear any breaking glass or crushing metal, and figured her car was probably going to be fine, such as it was. Marti looked around for the other car driver, but a man walking out of a store on the other side of the street caught her attention. It looked like Cliff Kogoya. She was about to wave when a truck drove past, and when her view cleared, the man was gone. I am seeing some weird shit today.

Marti shrugged, tossed her cigarette to the ground, and walked into Tomas Akello's office. Tomas's office was clean, modern, and uncluttered. Light gray walls and minimalist furnishings gave the office a cool, detached atmosphere. There was no secretary, so when Marti walked in, she was face to face with the man.

"How can I help you today?" Akello asked. It made him sound like he was about to take your French fry order.

"I'm Marti Starova, private investigator," she said as she sat in the smooth leather guest chair. "I've been hired to look into the death of Andreas Katsaros."

Akello leaned back in his chair and furrowed his brow. "How does his death bring you to my office, Ms. Starova?"

She did not want to tell him it was coded cum, so she said, "Can you tell me how much he hired you for?"

Akello held up his hand to stop Marti mid-sentence. "I can't tell you any information about my clients any more than you can tell me about yours," he said.

"New or old business?"

"None of your business."

Marti nodded. "I know. But I need to tell my client that I checked. Can you tell me–"

"No."

"Where I can pick up some cigarettes?" Marti finished. She held up her almost empty pack for him to see.

"Sorry about that. There's a convenience store at Thirty-ninth and Laird," he said.

Marti thanked Akello and headed down the street. He intimated that Andreas had been a client. That meant he wasn't hired by Elizabeth to divorce William Preston. Since he usually had female clients, Marti felt she could justify investigating Isabella and the possibility of divorce. It gave Isabella a motive, though she had no means. That's what hitmen were for.

Marti bought a pack of cigarettes from the store and sat on the curb, watching cars drive by. She frowned when she saw a black sedan drive by; she was sure for the fifth or sixth time. It was probably the Feds. She hoped it was real this time.

Marti scanned the area and decided an alley across the way looked like a good possibility. She wanted some alone time, without prying eyes. Marti trotted across the street, dodging a car that blasted its horn at her. She scanned the alley, and it looked good.

Marti walked past a small dumpster, plastic garbage cans, and a pile of rotting cardboard boxes. She wanted an area that was dry, rat-free and recessed. She settled for two out of three and retreated into a damp doorway. Pulling out an inhaler, Marti drew in as much Shadow as she could in one breath.

Holding her breath, she sunk down to the concrete and exhaled.

Chapter 27

The mid-morning light filtered through the streaky windows, casting a muted glow in Marti's office. She sat behind her desk, eyes unfixed as Shadow roamed through her mind. The mist outside clung to the cityscape, a somber shroud that matched the weight in the air. Papers and case files lay scattered, momentarily forgotten.

Marti was dirty, having passed out in the alley. When she woke up, her neck ached and her back was sore from lying on the ground. She had a vague sense that she ought to shower.

In the neighboring office, Lori immersed herself in organizing digital case files and tagging which ones to print for clients. A subdued silence replaced the usual hum of the office, acknowledging the shared awareness of the day's solemn purpose.

"Andreas Katsaros was a man of many mysteries," Marti said loudly, her voice echoing in the quiet office.

Lori nodded and stopped typing. She got up and walked to Marti's office, perching on the arm of a chair. "His company is a shell for Ari's cartel, but killing him did no harm against Ari. The Board of Directors took over without a hitch. So, personal?"

Marti shook her head. "Yeah. With the company, kill the top guy, and the next one just moves up to take his place. Did he have life insurance?"

"Yes, a million dollar policy that's almost ten years old. We could really use access to police records," Lori said, raising an eyebrow.

Marti leaned forward, her eyes gleaming with curiosity. "That would be fun, but too suspect for me to show up there again so soon. And I'm sure they have deleted Kane's account, so you can't just walk in and log into his of account. You well and truly have to hack in. But why kill Andreas in a crowded nightclub? It's not like it is easy to get in there. The hotel would have been the better place."

"Well, you did said there was security at the hotel. And you got into the club," Lori said. "You got in by hanging around outside and waiting for someone to take you in."

Marti snorted. "You have that all wrong. I got in by hanging around outside, looking hot, and waiting for someone to take me in."

"So we're looking for someone who's hot?"

"Piping hot," Marti laughed.

"Maybe they were already in there? And why isn't Isabella a suspect?"

"Heather said she was 'not in a position' to commit the crime. She was physically incapable. I think it means they found Isabella bound in the club. Isabella said she was blinded and could only tell it was Andreas by his smell."

"That's gross," Lori sighed.

"What? Can't you tell people by smell?"

Lori slipped into the chair and shook her head. "No, and I don't want to talk about that. You stink right now. What if it was Elizabeth who wanted revenge for being poor?"

"Or Henrick, who wanted him punished for having a second family. Or Katarina. Or Ria."

"Did Henrick know about them?"

"We don't know," Marti said. "This is a fucking mess."

Marti's fingers tapped rhythmically on her desk, her mind racing through the possibilities. "The way he was killed, a single stab wound to the chest, suggests something personal, a level of intimacy that goes beyond what we've found so far. We're missing something."

"Someone with a very deep-seated hatred like a spurned daughter? He had two," Lori said, her voice laced with a hint of disbelief.

"The calculated nature of the killing, the precision of the strike, points to someone who was intimately familiar with Andreas's movements. I just don't think Ria knew him like that. Not as Andreas," Marti explained.

Marti glanced at the clock, her fingers tapping rhythmically on the worn surface of her desk. The funeral of Andreas loomed ahead, a gathering that the women planned to attend from afar. She hated funerals.

"Yes, it's time," Lori said when she saw Marti looking.

Marti quickly cleaned up in the office shower, cleared her mind, and lit a cigarette. Both women headed to the car and arrived at the cemetery early. They stood under umbrellas at the edge of the walkway, watching. One gravedigger lowered a hose into the grave and the other started the pump. Muddy water flowed out of that grave and over and into the surrounding graves. It seemed to Marti that if the procession were to be delayed, they'd have to pump the water out again.

The paths between the rows of marble tombstones were pristine. No one returned to the graves after the first visit. Mournful strains of a distant siren echoed through the misty shroud, its melancholy melody intertwining with the soft patter of rain on umbrellas. The air was heavy with the scent of wet earth and the palpable weight of collective grief.

The mourners arrived and waited around the grave, waiting for Andreas's coffin. Ari Stirling stood surrounded by a group of men, chatting. Ari pointed toward Marti and Lori with his head, and in unison, the group of men looked at them and then turned away.

"Let's mingle," Marti said. Ari had promised Marti that she and Lori had access to question every Board member at the funeral. Those were the Board members, and that was the signal.

"Hi. I'm Marti Starova. I'm working for Ari Stirling. He suggested we have a word," Marti said to the first person she happened upon.

Lori headed to the opposite side of the crowd. "Hi. I'm Lori Harring. I'm working for Ari Stirling. He suggested we have a word," Lori said to a couple.

The questions began, and the answers flowed.

"I saw Andreas about a week ago when we had a casual chat. Nothing unusual. He didn't mention any concerns."

"We had our differences, but nothing that would make me want him dead. It's just business. If it's not him, it will just be the next guy."

"Enemies? Well, in our line of work, you make some. But nothing I'd think would lead to this."

"I was at home all night, alone. You can ask my neighbors if you need an alibi. I make a shit ton of noise. And I resent you asking."

"Financially, Andreas was stable. Personal life, who knows? We're not that close."

"I didn't notice anything unusual during the funeral ceremony. People were grieving. It looked legitimate."

"I heard some rumors, but nothing concrete. Nothing I will repeat. People talk, you know? It's just trash talking."

"Valuables? If he had any, he kept that stuff private. He didn't wear any flashy watches or carry expensive phones. Just an average guy, really."

"Unusual circumstances? Well, he seemed stressed lately, but who isn't?"

"Who might want to kill him? I don't know, you figure that out. That's your job."

"I was out of town that day. Can't be near a crime scene when you're miles away."

"He owed me money, but killing him? That's extreme. I'd prefer getting paid."

"We argued at the office a few days ago. Just some HR stuff. He owed me some overtime. Like two hundred dollars. Nothing that serious."

"I don't know much about his personal life. He kept it separate from work."

"I didn't see anyone acting suspicious. Everyone was mourning, as far as I could tell."

"Expressing ill will? Look, we all had our disagreements, but murder? That's a stretch."

"I don't know, but whoever it is has a target on their back. Ari will get them one way or another."

"Unusual circumstances? Not really. Same old routine, work and more work."

"I was at the back during the service. A few people cried, but nothing suspicious."

"It's a funeral, for God's sake. Show some respect."

Marti lit a cigarette and retreated to the parking lot, waiting for Lori. She picked a piece of tobacco from her tongue and flicked it to the ground. The answers she got were useless, and she hoped Lori did better.

Marti knew from the look on Lori's face as she approached. "Struck out?"

"Yes."

The rain continued its melancholic dance as Marti and Lori stood side by side under their umbrellas, the damp air clinging to their coats. Marti was frustrated. She looked at Lori, raindrops glistening on her coat, then looked beyond. "Feds."

Lori looked toward where Marti was looking, adjusting her umbrella. "Yes, I think so. It's hard to tell. Everyone is hiding their faces with umbrellas."

The distant murmur of the organ signaled the approaching pallbearers, a reminder of the purpose that had brought them together on this gloomy day. Marti ran a hand through her wet hair, her gaze fixed on the dark figures at the gathering.

"I'm sure neither side wants to be seen by the other. But it's a public space. Anyone can be here," Marti said, frustration clear in her voice.

Lori nodded, raindrops sliding down her umbrella. "We're missing something."

As the pallbearers came into view, the atmosphere shifted. The weight of unanswered questions remained, but beneath it was a respect for the dead. Marti and Lori watched in solemn silence as the casket approached, the rain a silent witness to the mysteries that lingered in the air.

Marti gazed somberly at those in attendance, her expression veiled by the overhang of her umbrella. The muted colors of the floral arrangements, a stark contrast to the gray backdrop of the day, whispered of the ephemeral nature of life and the inevitability of farewell.

The officiant's voice, steady yet tinged with a somber cadence, barely rose above the murmur of the attendees.

Everyone seemed to talk business to someone else. Only Henrick and Isabella might have been crying. In the rain, it was hard to tell.

Marti looked for Elizabeth and Ria, but they were not in attendance. It was a smart choice they did not attend.

A person on the periphery watched as the casket lowered. They, like everyone else, were hidden by an umbrella. Marti wondered if they were another child from another damned family. They tossed flowers into the grave. Some fell into the mucky water beside the casket and got sucked up by the water pump and spit out onto other graves.

"Who is that?" Lori asked. She, too, had seen the person.

Marti shook her head. "It's like I should know, but I just can't see a face."

As soon as the officiant concluded his eulogy, people dispersed. Henrick and Isabella were the first to leave, heading to an elegant black car that waited nearby for them. For once, Henrick didn't have his phone in his hand.

Then Ari and his crew left in three cars. The other hangers-on left in clusters, leaving Marti and Lori to watch the last of them go.

As the rain stopped, they scanned the line of cars. Black cars, silver cars, white cars. Only one car, a white one, needed a wash. The driver took the long way around, skipping past the line to rush out.

"I'd suggest going for a coffee, but that didn't work out so well the last time," Lori said as they got into the car. Marti lit a cigarette and laughed. The rain slowed.

"That's the truth. You can wash my car again, if you want," Marti said.

Lori punched her in the arm. "You wish."

"I do. But let's try a coffee again. I'm sure there won't be a wild gun fight. The first place we find where there's parking?"

Lori agreed, and they drove out of the cemetery. The rain finally stopped.

Chapter 28

The rain had stopped pouring down, and the sun's dull rays broke through the clouds. It took just fifteen minutes to spot a place. Marti eyed a parking spot on the street and parked. There was no parking fight this time, no need to smash up her car. No need for her gun. "We just passed a patio. Let's actually sit outside in the sun and have a drink."

"In the sun?" Lori asked as she got out of the car. "I'd always imagined you were a vampire, and you'd burn up in the sun."

They got out of the car, Marti leaving her gun in the glove compartment. She had become too paranoid in public, had too many hallucinations to trust herself. She hated the thought of shooting Lori by accident.

The women walked the half block to the patio Marti had seen. The patio transformed into a glistening haven, kissed by the aftermath of the downpour that had drowned the funeral. It infused the air with the familiar aroma of wet pavement and the invigorating scent of garbage-soaked streets.

The patio, adorned with sleek metal tables and chairs, glistened under the sunlight, the raindrops on surfaces catching the beams and casting a radiant sparkle. Puddles formed on the ground, reflecting the surrounding cityscape like liquid mirrors, adding an ethereal quality to the scene. "Well, this is almost beautiful," Marti said as they passed the patio fence.

Since the chairs had been tilted in the rain, all we had to do was sit them back properly and give them a quick wipe. It felt good to sit.

The wet sidewalk resonated with the rhythmic tap-tap of footsteps, creating a melodic backdrop to the bustling city life. The occasional passing taxi sent ripples through the puddles, creating miniature waves that dance with the sun's reflection.

Marti and Lori sat beneath a large awning and placed their order. The server nodded silently and headed inside.

A rainbow of colors emerged as the sun catches on rain-soaked awnings and the vibrant blooms of flowers.

The city skyline, washed clean by the rain, stood tall and majestic, its buildings gleaming in the newfound clarity.

"Geez, it's kind of surreal. Almost magical," Lori said, looking around.

"You noticed, huh? Me too. Almost too good to be true."

"Don't you dare jinx this, Martina Starova!" Lori laughed.

Marti and Lori felt lucky, sitting street side with two hot Vietnamese coffees. Traffic passed them slowly, creeping along the street. Engines hummed, horns honked, drivers yelled.

"I don't buy Elizabeth as the villain here," Lori said.

"Agreed. When we told her about William…wow. That was not fake," Marti said. She sipped her coffee, made sweet with condensed milk. "Heather said Elizabeth was out for a walk without her phone. That sucks as an alibi."

"Should we be re-interviewing her? Following up to see if anyone actually saw her?" Lori asked.

Marti shook her head. "If we find out who really killed him, then her lack of an alibi doesn't matter. No reason to waste time on her," Marti said.

"Waste time? That's harsh. Who else have we got? Is-abella and Henrick. Katarina. Ria. Who else?" Lori said. "Maybe there's another family we don't know about."

"A third family? Yeah. I'm not liking it at all," Marti said. She lit a cigarette and watched the breeze carry away the smoke. "But I guess people will start to come out of the woodwork now that his death is public news."

"Marti! Hey, Marti!"

Rat, a friend of Marti's, shuffled up to the pair.

"Hey, Rat! What's up?"

"Marti, my favorite investigator! How's life treating you? Hi, uh, hi, uh, hi." It was as close to remembering Lori's name as Rat could muster.

"Surviving the chaos, as always. What about you?"

"You know, the usual grind. Say, you wouldn't have an extra inhaler, would you? The prices are insane now," he said.

"Sorry Rat, I'm clean. Feds arrested me the other day and took everything. Need some money?" Marti asked. Lori shot her a look, but Marti ignored it. "I can't pay for a whole one, but I can throw a hundred your way."

"Really? That'd be a lifesaver. Appreciate it, Marti. That will get me a hit or two."

Marti pulled out a few bills and handed them to Rat. "Here. Stay safe man, the Feds are up our asses right now." She hoped Heather was listening in.

Horns honked, and a siren wailed distantly. An urban opera of distress. The wail of a car horn was very close. Marti's heart clenched. Was this real?

Her gaze traced the path of danger, landing on a car spiraling out of control towards them–a metallic beast charging without restraint. A jolt of primitive fear coupled with roiling adrenaline drowned out the world around her. It was as if time had thickened, stretching each second into an eternity as she watched their doom approach. It was all instinct now, and everything went silent.

Her hand trembled as it instinctively shot out across the table to clutch Lori by her coat. The fearful exchange in their eyes said more than any words ever could–they were ensnared in this dance with death together.

With a force born from the survival instinct that lay dormant in all humanity until truly needed, Marti tugged Lori towards her. Their bodies fell to the cool concrete patio ground at once, Lori's terrified whimper swallowed up by the harsh screech of protesting tires. Toward the wall!

At that moment, Marti tasted the bitterness of fear and smelled the sharp tang of exhaust fumes mixed with their spilled coffee. The silence that followed was more profound than any cathedral's hush.

Flashes of destruction tore through Marti's mind, each one more brutal than the last. Glass shattered, blood spilled, metal twisted, plastic melted, and asphalt cracked in her vision. With terrifying speed, these images became like lightning-fast flashcards, each one pushing her closer to the edge of sanity. Suddenly, a tire grazed her face, leaving a searing mark and a trail of rubber. Before she could process this new threat, the deafening sound of a car colliding with a wall echoed in her ears, drowning out all rational thought. Darkness descended upon Marti as she saw a thick, viscous fluid dripping onto the ground beside her. Its surface shimmered with an otherworldly rainbow-like sheen as it slowly spread towards her like a creeping monster.

A heavy and acrid scent filled the air: a mix of chemicals, with notes of petroleum and a hint of burned undertones. Like a cheap whiskey, Marti thought.

Chapter 29

An excruciating, high-pitched screech that seemed to pierce through her eardrums assaulted Marti's senses. A blanket of impenetrable darkness consumed her vision, leaving her disoriented and vulnerable. With a sharp intake of breath, Marti's mind clawed its way back to consciousness as she frantically tested the movement of her limbs. Relieved to find nothing missing, she was suddenly bombarded with urgent voices that seem to shout incoherently. As she blinked away the residual darkness, Marti found herself face to face with a stranger whose features were twisted with fear and concern.

Marti's head snapped towards the sound of crying, her heart a jackhammer. Lori, tears streaming down her face, held her arm in pain. Marti watched as Lori slowly sat up.

The sound of her cry brought Marti's consciousness to the fore. At that moment, she knew Lori was alive and intact. A wave of relief wash over her like a flood cooling the flames of Hell.

Without hesitation, Marti inched along the sidewalk, her focus solely on reaching Lori and embracing her. Every inch felt like a triumph. When she finally reached her, Marti sat up and pulled Lori into her arms, holding her tight and whispering soothing words into her ear.

As they clung to each other, Marti could feel Lori's trembling body relax and her sobs turn into gentle hiccups. In that moment, nothing else mattered but the two of them, safe and together.

Marti pulled away and looked into Lori's red-rimmed eyes, her heart aching at the sight. Without a word, she reached into her pocket and pulled out a crumpled tissue, handing it to Lori with a small smile.

Lori took it gratefully and wiped her tears, her smile returning to her face.

"Holy fuck! Are you okay?" someone screamed in Marti's face.

"Did you see that bastard? Just drove away! That piece of shit won't get far," shouted another. Marti pushed people aside.

"Hey." It was the best Marti could manage.

Lori looked at her and blinked a few more tears. "Ow," she said, slightly moving her arm.

"Bleeding?"

"No. You?"

"Don't think so. But I think we both need the hospital," Marti said. "Did anyone call an ambulance? No? Assholes." Marti made her way slowly up to her feet and pulled her phone from her pocket. Despite being cracked, the phone still worked. She called for emergency services for herself and Lori, and an old man on the sidewalk who had also been hit. Somehow, Rat had scurried away in time.

"Help me stand up," Lori said, reaching out her hand.

As Marti helped Lori to her feet, she cursed. "Fucking coffee. I am starting to really hate coffee. Did anyone see what happened?"

"Some guy drove up on the sidewalk. I think he might have got hit first, pushed up. Then he took off, but I think someone went after him."

"No way. He was aiming. Drove straight up."

"Anyone get a plate?"

"It didn't have one. Probably a Nomad." The bystander was suggesting the car was an off-the-books taxi. With no plates and freewheeler drivers, Nomads were the bane of

Falls City. Marti often used them because they reported nothing to the police.

"Did you see anything?" Marti asked.

"Light, maybe silver. Small. That's all," Lori answered.

The call of a siren broke through the hum of the city.

It took just three minutes for Marti, Lori, and Walter, the old man, to arrive at the hospital. Just long enough for Walter to look out the ambulance window and ask where the fuck they were going. Where the fuck did he think they were going?

Marti footed the bill for the shared ambulance. Marti also fronted Walter a $5,000 credit with the hospital.

"You're an angel," he said as they wheeled him away into a treatment room.

Marti laughed. "I've been called a lot of things, Walter. I think that's a new one. Good luck."

"You are an angel," Lori said with a soft smile. She stroked Marti's face.

"Nice try. You have to pay your own bill. I'm only covering Walter. Joke! Joke! Get that look off your face," Marti said. They were handed tickets: Numbers 178 and 179. Marti looked at the service board: 170. Soon.

Medical treatment at hospitals was largely automated, with artificial intelligence and robotics taking over mundane complaints like broken bones, stomach aches and snotty noises. The tech made it more affordable than ever to get hit by a car.

It also meant there were few medical personnel in an emergency room. The real money was in catering to the whims of the extremely wealthy who wanted to live forever. They'd pay for snake oil if they thought it would give them another day on this dumpster fire of a world.

Marti's gaze roamed the waiting area, looking for a place for them to sit. One vacant seat was covered in vomit. A second seat a little further down was next to a man who looked like it was his vomit.

She sighed and ushered Lori to a space on the wall. At least they could lean. "How hurt are you?" she asked.

Lori moved her shoulder slightly, then her elbow. She winced. "I'll need a scan to be sure, but it hurts. Maybe surgery?" Marti nodded. It shouldn't take long for the scans: they were fully automated. "How about you?" Lori asked.

"Just the scan, I think."

"Number 178, please step to the scan," said the automated voice. Marti gave Lori the ticket and ushered her to the scan. Lori stepped into the metal tube and the door closed. Fifteen seconds later, she stepped out and picked up her printout.

"Number 179, please step to the scan," said the automated voice. It was Marti's turn, and seconds later, she held her printout.

"Number 180, please step to the scan," said the automated voice.

Someone stood up clutching a ticket, and Marti ushered Lori to the now vacant seat. "Mine is internal and external bruising. Fentafill prescription. Party time. What about yours?" Marti asked.

"A SnapRepair. You'll wait for me, right?" The SnapRepair procedure would take half an hour once they took her in. Tiny, bio-compatible high-tech splints would be strategically positioned around the fracture. The SnapRepair system's robotic arms would meticulously align the fractured segments under the watchful eye of the human surgeon. Lori would receive a specialized healing agent, comprising nanomaterials and growth factors, to expedite the natural healing process.

"Number 178, please step to room 47B," said the automated voice.

"Of course I'll wait," Marti said. "Go before you lose your spot." Lori walked to room 47B and Marti took her chair. Soon enough her nerves got the better of her, and she stepped outside for a cigarette: even she knew not to smoke in a hospital. She inhaled deeply, thinking about the car. Lori said it was small and light colored, maybe silver. A witness said it was unplated. It wasn't much to go on. She'd have to get a report from a sympathetic traffic cop. Except she didn't know one.

Marti was almost finished with her cigarette when a police cruiser arrived, accompanying a black car. Heather Blair stepped out of the black car, and two uniformed officers stood behind her.

"What brings you here?" Heather asked with a smile.

Marti flicked her butt away and exhaled. Heather walked up to Marti and stood right in front of her, and gave a luxurious smile. Marti was not in the mood.

"What can I do for you and your dogs?" Marti said, motioning with her head toward the uniformed officers.

"Dogs? What brought that on?"

"A Nomad ran Lori and me over. I'm not in a good mood."

Heather sighed and looked up at the sky. "Why me?"

Chapter 30

Heather Blair stood at the entrance of the emergency department, nodding as she listened to Marti. "Let's go over here. We're here for the car incident."

As they walked along the side of the building, Marti asked the obvious question. "Why are the Feds interested in a car crash?"

"Uh uh," Heather said, holding her finger to her lips. She looked around and moved Marti toward a back corner. "Gentlemen, I'll be a moment," she said, pointing for the officers to stay.

Heather turned her back so no one but Marti could see her speaking. In a low voice, she said, "The other person injured is my concern. Not that you and your secretary aren't important. But he's my interest."

"Walter? Why?" Marti asked. She knew she wouldn't hear a decent answer, but she had to ask.

"You know his name?" Heather was shocked.

"His first name, yeah."

Heather sighed. "Walter is assisting us with a case. That's all I can say."

Marti narrowed her eyes, her mind racing. "Are you saying he was the target? That someone attacked him on purpose and we were just collateral?"

Heather nodded and shrugged. "That's what I believe."

Marti stared at her for a moment. If Walter was involved in a federal case in Falls City, it was an extensive investigation.

"Fuck. Who is Walter? I paid for part of his hospital bill," she said.

"No, no, no." Heather shook her head vehemently. "Cancel it. Correct it. Do not be associated with him. At all. Can you do that?"

"Yeah." Marti frowned. "Fuck. Is there anything you can tell me other than that?"

Heather shook her head. "Just separate yourself from Walter. Make sure your friend is okay. Forget his name. Go home. You'll be fine. Okay?"

Marti nodded. Heather turned to go, but turned back. "Call me. Not about this. For a drink. Yes?" Marti nodded again and watched as Heather walked away. Nice ass.

Less than an hour ago, Marti had paid $5,000 into Walter's hospital account. Heather just told her that Walter was a police informant of some kind, and Marti needed to untangle herself from her previous act of kindness. She couldn't let anyone know she had purposely paid for his treatment.

Marti sighed and headed to Accounts Payable to gaslight the clerk. She needed the funds credited to her account, and she needed the clerk to think he was the one responsible for the mistake. Then, if anyone asked, it was a clerical error for Marti's money to be associated with Walter.

"Hi, I'm Martina Starova. I just paid a hospital credit less than an hour ago." She handed over her identification.

"Yes, ma'am, how can I help you?" he asked.

Marti checked his name tag. "Simon, I checked my account at the kiosk. There is no record of the $5,000 I paid on my account," Marti said. She fiercely rubbed her face to make it turn red.

Her assertion shocked Simon, and he immediately looked at her account. "That's right, there is no credit on your account."

"Where did my $5,000 go?" Marti asked with panic in her voice. "Do you have a record of me paying the credit? I can't believe this. How could the system make this kind of mistake?" Marti played up her hysteria, falling dramatically into a chair. "I don't have that kind of money! I need it back. I need the credit on my account." She clutched at the imaginary pearls around her neck.

"I'm sorry, let me check," Simon said. After a few clicks, he nodded. "I can see you paid a $5,000 credit for a Walter Lewis."

"No, no, no. I don't know who that is. Walter Lewis? Who is that? My money should be on my account. Simon, what happened here? Where is my money? Why are you stealing it and giving it to a stranger?" Marti spoke quickly, adding to the tension and pressure.

"Th-This shows you signed off on the payment. I didn't steal it," Simon said.

"Oh no! I can't pay that kind of money for a stranger," Marti said, her voice rising. "How could you do this to me?"

"I didn't do anything," he said defensively.

"Well, I didn't do this either! Can you please transfer it back to my account? What a terrible mistake." Marti pretended to cry. "Oh. My. God!" Marti shouted as she looked around. She knew that getting others interested in her drama would make Simon more likely to give in.

Panicked, Simon tried to calm Marti. "Please don't cry. Let me... Shh. Please stop." People were looking at the fuss Marti was creating. "Let me take care of this. Just give me a second. And... There. Done. I have credited your $5,000 to your account. Please stop crying," Simon begged.

"Oh thank you Simon," Marti said with a sickly sweetness. "You've saved me. Thank you so much. Everyone? He was so helpful." Marti thanked him a few more times.

Once it was settled, and the money was applied to Marti's account, she impassively headed back to the waiting area. Lori was still being treated.

Marti rolled the light car, silver car, maybe silver, around in her head. A small light...white. White car. Damn! A white car was at the center of it all: the patio attack, the outsider at the funeral, the car at the bodega. Marti looked up the phone number for the shop near her home. "Carlos? It's Marti. I was at your store two days ago. You let me leave by the back door."

"Oh yes! I remember. What about it?" Carlos asked.

"Do you still have the surveillance video? From the outside front of the store?"

"Two days ago? Yes, I keep it for a week. You want it?"

"Yes please. I'll send you a link so you can upload it. I'll send you $100 for your troubles," Marti said. She stepped outside again for a cigarette. Rubbing her temples, she tried to figure out her next steps. Her phone buzzed.

Where are you? Lori messaged.

Smoking. Coming in, Marti responded. She took one last drag, tossed the cigarette away, and exhaled a cloud of smoke as she walked in.

"I thought you'd left me for a minute," Lori said as Marti sidled up to her.

"Never. You all set?"

"I still have to pay," Lori said.

"Allow me, please," Marti said with a flourish. She tapped in Lori's patient number and a bill of $34,726 came up. Marti held her credit against the reader and paid the bill. She repeated it for her own account and paid the remaining $9,528.

"How were you? Are you feeling $35,000 better?" Marti asked as they walked out of the hospital.

"How am I? Well, I did just get hit by a car," Lori said.

"Yeah, rough day at the office." Marti looked around at the traffic. She studied every car. She checked out every person walking by. "I want to take you home," Marti said as she angled Lori toward the taxi stand outside the hospital.

"Pardon me?" Lori said. She was clearly shocked.

"I meant, I want to be in the cab with you and make sure you get home safe. Not that I want to fuck you," Marti said.

Lori stopped walking. "You don't want to fuck me?"

"Oh for–I mean, look, I think we were the targets. Maybe me, maybe you, maybe both of us. Maybe Walter fucking Lewis. Let me take you back to your place. Make sure you're okay. Okay?"

Lori looked at Marti's worried face and nodded. "Okay. Who are Walter and Lewis, and where are they fucking?"

Chapter 31

Marti and Lori stood in the elevator, waiting for the doors to close. Marti's heart was pounding, and she felt the walls closing in on her. It was only the doors closing, but it felt like so much more. She tried to take deep breaths, but it was no use. She was trapped in a small metal box with no way out.

Lori looked at Marti and smiled. "You're so funny when you're scared," she said. Lori always found it funny when Marti got claustrophobic. She didn't understand why Marti was so afraid of small spaces, but she found it entertaining to watch her panic.

Marti didn't find it funny at all. She was terrified and felt like she was suffocating. She wanted to get out of the elevator as soon as possible. The elevator ascended. Marti felt sick to her stomach. She closed her eyes and tried to focus on her breathing.

Lori watched Marti with amusement. She couldn't believe that her friend was so afraid of something as mundane as an elevator. She thought it was ridiculous, maybe even a put-on.

The elevator reached the 18th floor, and the doors opened. Marti rushed out of the elevator, gasping for air. Lori followed behind her, still laughing.

"You're such a scaredy-cat," Lori said.

"You're annoying me and you're lucky I need you on my side," Marti said as her heart rate returned to normal.

"Finally, something truthful from you," Lori joked as she unlocked the apartment door.

Lori's home was stunning. It had floor-length windows on two walls. One overlooked the city center and the other, Chata Falls. Rustic hundred-year-old brickwork framed the windows. The floor was polished concrete. Old tin tiles covered the high ceiling.

The front door opened to the kitchen, with the bedroom and living space all in one large room. One door lead to the bathroom, another to a closet.

"Damn," Marti said as she walked inside. "How much am I paying you?"

Lori laughed. "Just enough. But this year, I'm getting a huge end-of-year bonus. To make up for getting shot and breaking my arm. Boots off. Have a seat," she said, gesturing to the two club chairs near the city view window.

"Drink?" Lori asked as she pulled a bottle of orange juice from the fridge.

"Ugh, orange juice? No thanks," Marti said as she took her boots off and pulled her hoodie over her head.

Lori laughed. "The juice is for me. I have whiskey."

"Then yes, whiskey for me." Marti knew Lori didn't drink whiskey. It meant she'd bought the bottle for guests. Like her.

"So what makes you think this might have been a targeted attack?" Lori said. She handed Marti her drink and sat down opposite.

"I spoke with Agent Blair. She arrived at the hospital, telling me Walter was the target."

"Walter? That sweet old man?"

"Heather freaked out when she heard I knew his first name. Said I had to take back the credit I gave him at the hospital, forget I ever met him. But the hospital clerk told me his full name is Walter Lewis," Marti said.

Lori got her laptop and returned to her seat. "Let's find out. 'Walter Lewis arrested', and…search. Oh, my."

Marti got up and moved to sit on the arm of Lori's chair. She took a drink and watched as Lori scrolled the broadsheet news coverage of Walter Lewis.

A year ago, the Feds had arrested Walter for misappropriating funds from a political action committee. He absconded with three million, fled to another country, was extradited and finally turned state's evidence against the candidate. The candidate was running for Governor.

"Fuck. That's amazing. No wonder Heather was so freaked out," Marti said.

"So if someone drove onto the sidewalk on purpose, he really might have been the target," Lori said.

"Mind if I smoke?"

"Yes, I mind. Let's step outside on the patio," Lori said.

"All this and a patio too? I think I have to pay myself as much as I pay you."

They sat outside under a glass overhang, out of the rain, to continue the conversation.

"The car accident... no, let's call it an attack. The car attack was too amateurish to have had Walter as the target," Marti said, drawing on her cigarette.

"Why?"

"Because he is still alive. If he was the target, they'd have shot him in the head."

"Well, what makes you think we were the target? That it wasn't actually an accident, and the guy fled the scene?" Lori asked.

"Heather thinks Elizabeth killed Andreas. William. Frank. Whatever the fuck his other name is," Marti said through a hazy cloud of smoke. "She's wrong. I guarantee she's wrong. I don't know how long she has been with the Feds, but I think she's kind of new. Kind of naïve. And I think she's wrong about Walter being the target."

Marti looked around for a place to stub out her cigarette, and the best she could do was hold it up to Lori. "Put it out on the ground and keep the butt."

Marti nodded. "The white car. Not silver. White. A white car for the attack, a white car for the unknown person at the funeral. And I didn't tell you this, but a white car was following me earlier this week. Carlos saw it at his bodega."

"Why didn't you say something?" Lori asked. She kicked her leg out toward Marti.

Marti drained the last of her whiskey. "I thought Carlos was being paranoid. He's the one who noticed, not me. He's sending me surveillance footage. I doubt it will help us much. But if I'm the target..."

"There are probably a hundred people who want to see you dead, Marti," Lori said. "Now, Dan Devall said you are safe from his people. And Kevin Gardner has nothing against you, so it probably wasn't him. And not Ari's people. But almost anyone else."

"There has been some crazy shit going on between those three. Someone's after Ari, I'm sure. Maybe there's a new player? Someone who knows I can survive all three of those fuckers," Marti said as she pointed to the idea like it was standing right in front of her.

"You think there's a new crew in town?" Lori asked with genuine concern on her face.

Marti looked at the ceiling while she thought, then shook her head. "If it was organized crime, it would have been a shot to the head. This is something else. Someone, an amateur, just a civilian, with something personal against me."

"Oh geez, that's a big list," Lori said. "How do you know I wasn't the target?"

Marti's face clouded over. "That's the thing. It could be you. You've been doing a lot more public work. Maybe it is about you. A minor case, not anything deserving of an assassination, but some regular person who hired us and is pissed off at you," Marti said.

Lori's breath caught in her throat as Marti's words hung in the air. The weight of the thought hit her like a sudden storm, leaving her momentarily breathless. Her eyes widened, searching Marti's face for any sign of disbelief or uncertainty, but the gravity in Marti's expression mirrored the seriousness of the situation.

"I mean, if you haven't noticed, it really seems like someone wants us dead."

"Don't say that. It's not about us," Lori said.

"It is about us."

"We don't know that."

"We can never know that, Lori. That's just a shitty part of working with me. It isn't the first time. It's just the most recent."

A surge of adrenaline sent a shiver down Lori's spine, her thoughts racing through a labyrinth of fear and disbelief. The notion that someone might try to end her life felt like a surreal nightmare, a twist in the plot she hadn't seen coming. Her chest tightened, a sinking feeling of vulnerability settling in.

Lori's gaze flickered around the room, as if expecting shadows to come after her.

"Marti, are you sure about this?" Lori's voice wavered, a mix of anxiety and a desperate need for reassurance. Everything seemed to close in.

"I think that until we have an answer, you need to be extra cautious. Maybe stop coming into work, start working from home," Marti said.

"Oh my God, what if they know where I live? What if they come here?" Lori cried out.

Lori sobbed, her shoulders trembling as tears streamed down her cheeks. Marti leaped up and placed a reassuring hand on Lori's back, offering a quiet presence amid the storm. "Shh. Lori, we'll figure this out. I won't let anything happen to you," Marti whispered. "Come on, let's go inside."

They walked in and Lori double checked the lock on the patio door. She was rattled, and sat on the edge of the bed trembling. "You're shivering," Marti said, sitting beside her and putting her arm around Lori's shoulder. Marti felt a thrill run through her body. She was close to Lori, and could feel her lust building. Damn it Marti, stop that shit! she thought.

"Lie down, relax. Under the covers. You've been through a lot today," Marti said as she pulled back the covers. Lori wiped tears from her face and climbed into bed. Marti passed her tissues and pulled the covers up.

"No, Marti. Don't leave. Stay with me, please," Lori said. She pulled back the covers and scooted over, making room for Marti.

Marti sighed as the familiar burn of lust ran from her stomach to her groin. She ran her hands over her stomach, trying to quench her desire. She shook her head.

"Marti, please. I don't want to be alone tonight," Lori begged.

"I've told you before, I can't touch you. I'm no good. I ruin everything," Marti said. She was trying desperately to keep desire out of her voice, to stop the blood from rushing to her face.

"So don't touch me. Sit beside me. Just...hold me," Lori said, holding her breath. She watched Marti as she got into the bed beside her. Lori exhaled, relieved. She leaned back and smiled at Marti. "Tell me what you would do if you could touch me."

Marti smiled, and stayed hummed softly, waiting for Lori to fall asleep.

Chapter 32

The industrial area of Falls City sprawled out like a forgotten relic of the city's past, a maze of dimly lit streets and dodgy warehouses. Marti navigated her car along the pitted road, raindrops shouting out their secrets in a melancholic rhythm on the roof.

Marti had spent the night at Lori's, having given her a special bedtime story and fallen asleep beside her. She woke before the sun was up. Her first cigarette of the morning was on Lori's patio, watching her sleep. She didn't stay much longer, but instead creeped out quietly, sat in her car, and planned her morning. And now here she was, driving around Falls City.

The murky silhouette of a car repair shop emerged, its flickering neon sign barely illuminating the entrance.

Stepping out into the damp air, Marti approached the shop, her hoodie pulled up against the drizzle. A reluctant employee behind the counter eyed her suspiciously as she inquired about a small white car with front end damage. "We have no white cars," he grumbled, a cigarette dangling from the corner of his mouth.

Marti leaned in, her tone low and, she hoped, persuasive. "A little white car, real inconspicuous. Might've had a run-in with a wall lately."

The unwilling mechanic scratched his scruffy beard, glancing around before shaking his head. "Lady, we fix cars. We ain't into keeping tabs on 'em. No small white cars here, damaged or not."

"Fine. Fine. You see my car? See the damage? Ballpark figure."

He looked out of the open bay door at Marti's car. "Five crisp."

She shook her head. She wasn't paying that kind of money. Undeterred, Marti slipped a business card onto the filthy counter. "In case you hear something through the grapevine. It's in your interest to let me know."

"Cash reward?"

"Yeah, cash reward," she answered. With that, she melted back into the rain-soaked day.

The search for the white car had put the investigation into Andreas's murder on the back burner. Andreas was already dead. He wouldn't mind waiting a little.

Marti continued to navigate the streets, the purr of her engine mingling with the urban symphony. She pulled up to another car repair shop, the peeling sign above whispering tales of years gone by. Stepping out into the gritty air, she approached the counter where a mechanic, clad in oil-stained coveralls, eyed her with a wary curiosity. His name tag read 'Mike.'

"Morning, Mike. Got a question for you. Looking for a small white car, front end damage. Have you seen it?" Marti asked.

Mike glanced up from a grimy clipboard, skepticism etched on his weathered face. "Maybe I have, maybe I haven't. What's in it for me if I spill?"

For fuck's sake, everyone wants money. "One hundred to see the car. Nothing if you don't have a small white car," Marti snapped.

"We've got three white cars," Mike said with a smile. "Three hundred."

"It would have arrived recently."

Mike shrugged. "I don't know when shit arrives. Three hundred."

Marti sighed and gave him $300 in credit. Mike nodded and motioned with his head to the cars behind the shop. "Knock yourself out."

Walking out of the shop, Marti scanned the area. As she circled the cars, she found a small, badly damaged white car. She noted the VIN and moved on to the next white car, and the next white car. She looked over her shoulder. Mike was watching her, a large wrench in his hands.

"How much to repair my car?" she asked.

Mike walked to her car, circled it, and said, "Eight thousand, including a new paint job."

She gave him a silent nod as she got into her car. On to the next shop.

Marti figured she could skip the legitimate repair garages: they would keep meticulous records and demand insurance information. With two down, Marti had five more shops to go. Her years as a cop meant she knew the questionable places to go. She hoped that nothing new had popped up without her noticing.

Within a few hours, Marti had seven VINs for seven small white cars in for repair. Now it was time for her own car. The quoted prices for repair were too high. It was time to trade.

Marti knew the best neighborhood for shady car deals was Ironwood. spied a car lot and pulled in. It was the corner of a parking lot, taken over by 'Sally's Super Sales.' There were a dozen cars for sale. Marti needed a car, and she preferred something cheap.

As Marti stepped out of her bashed up car, her eyes scanned the small car sales lot. The air was charged with the scent of freshly polished metal and deceit, an intoxicating mix that only added to Marti's excitement.

Sally, the proprietor of this automotive paradise, greeted Marti with a warm smile as she approached a new potential client.

Marti's eyes flitted from car to car, her heart quickening with anticipation. As she approached the first car, a sleek silver coupe, Marti marveled at its aerodynamic curves and polished exterior. She mentally envisioned herself zipping down the open road, wind whipping through her hair, as she embraced the freedom that this sporty machine offered.

But it was not only the silver coupe that enticed her. A vibrant blue sedan sat a few paces away, exuding an air of sophistication and elegance. Its luxurious leather seats seemed to invite Marti into their plush embrace, promising comfort and refinement on every journey.

Next to the blue sedan stood a rugged SUV with a gleaming black exterior, its sturdy frame ready to conquer even the most treacherous terrains. Marti imagined herself embarking on thrilling off-road adventures, conquering mountains and valleys with this powerful beast by her side.

But Falls City had mountains called garbage and valleys called gutters. The only off-road adventure would be to drive through roads so full of potholes it felt like a rally.

With Sally at her side, Marti approached a sporty red car. Its body had weathered the years with grace, the paint still gleaming like liquid fire in the rain. She could almost hear its engine purring softly as if inviting her to take it for a joyride.

Sally began her patter. "I'm thrilled to tell you about this sporty red car you're interested in. We call it the 'Thunder XTRA.' Despite being nine years old, this car has proven to be a true powerhouse over the years. The Thunder XTRA boasts a stunning red exterior that turns heads wherever it goes. Guys will stare while you drive past. While it's not a convertible, the sleek and aerodynamic design gives it an edgy, sporty look that captures the essence of speed and performance. Besides, convertibles don't work well in Falls City."

Marti rolled her eyes when Sally suggested it would draw attention. "Stop, you're right. I just want a car that will blend in. How about that black one?"

"Yes, absolutely, the black Harrisburg Lux. Very fitting for this city. Now, let's talk about its impressive mileage.

With a hundred thousand miles on the odometer, this car has truly stood the test of time. Its robust engineering and durable components make it a reliable choice for those who appreciate both style and substance. Available by lease only."

Marti knew that meant they did not have a title for it, and it could be repossessed. "Look, I know this is all bullshit. Okay? I just want a clean title. I will be checking."

Sally gave her a look. "Clean title? Okay. The Storm 4G. Black, average looking. Eight years old, one hundred and ten thousand miles on it. Clean title. Despite its age and mileage, our expert team has meticulously examined the Storm 4G. It's a strong contender. Clean title, fully repaired. Warrantied for a year."

Marti looked carefully at the VIN. She could see that the metal VIN plate was a little crooked: a sure sign the original had been removed and a new, registered VIN had been put on. Clean enough.

The negotiations began, but Marti ended them quickly. "Twenty thousand, credit. Or twelve thousand cash plus my car as a trade-in. Clean title." Although cash was not actual, physical cash, it was an untraceable digital transaction as good as cash. And her car had a clean title.

"Twelve thousand plus trade. She's all yours."

Marti thanked Sally and transferred everything from her old car to her new car. Sally was kind enough to transfer the plates. "Registration and insurance are up to you," Sally said.

"Always. Immediate transfer?"

"Immediate transfer," Sally agreed.

Marti paid and drove off the lot in her Storm 4G. She'd ask Lori to verify the title, change the registration and insurance. It was time to head to the office. She hoped it wouldn't be weird.

Chapter 33

On her way to the office, and to see Lori for the first time since the apartment, she received a message from Ha-Yoon:

"I have a gift for you. Come and go." Marti hoped it had something to do with Andreas and headed over to the coroner's office before her own office.

Marti arrived and parked in the guest parking. When Ha-Yoon said 'come and go,' it wasn't a sexual invitation. It meant whatever it was would take just minutes, and she expected Marti to leave quickly.

Marti dashed through the rain and into the building. Ha-Yoon beamed when she saw her. She was on the phone and pointed to a bag behind her. Marti reached over the desk and grabbed a bag. Ha-Yoon nodded. Marti looked inside.

It was a brand new black leather jacket.

"No way!" Marti whispered in excitement. She pulled it out. The rich aroma of leather enveloped her as she held it close to her face, her fingers instinctively reaching out to graze the smooth surface of the gift.

Marti couldn't resist the allure of the jacket's symphony of shadows and sheen. She held it to the light. The jacket, cool to the touch, whispered promises of adventure and pleasure.

Marti hesitated for a moment before slipping her arms into the sleeves. The leather embraced her like a second skin, the slight creaking sound echoing the jacket's resistance to conform.

The black leather, adorned with subtle creases and scars, caught the light in a dance of light and dark. She ran her fingers over the surface, tracing the contours of zippers and seams. The creak of leather softened as she moved, the jacket settling into a tailored embrace.

Marti gave a big smile to Ha-Yoon and in return, Ha-Yoon pointed to her left shoulder, the jacket, and her left shoulder again. Marti looked down and saw a small stain. She threw her head back and silently laughed. Ha-Yoon had christened the jacket already. Marti gave the spot a quick kiss. Ha-Yoon winked and turned away, paying full attention to the phone call.

Marti bounded out of the coroner's office, almost giddy, and jumped into her car. "Fuck yeah!" Marti shouted as she drove to her office.

She walked in wearing the jacket.

"A new jacket?" Lori said.

"It's been used. Apparently."

Lori's eyes narrowed. She stopped her typing and looked fully at Marti. Her eyes roamed the jacket, searching for rips, tears, or distress. She saw only a faint mark on the shoulder.

"Already stained, I see," Lori said.

Marti grunted in the affirmative.

"Where'd you get it? Steal it from a little old lady?"

"Hmm, yeah. A little old lady," Marti said. She lit a cigarette and sat down.

"You stole it then?" Lori raised an eyebrow and tilted her head. A look of disapproval cast over her face.

"I think it was some kind of payment for services rendered," Marti said. She took a strong drag off her cigarette and looked at her arm through the smoke. This was beautiful leather.

"You're playing with me," Lori said.

"I've told you before, that will not happen."

Lori flicked her pen at Marti and shook her head. "You're terrible."

"I've told you that before, too. It was a gift," Marti said. She tapped her shoulder. "Ha-Yoon."

"Oh Marti, you really are rotten. You could have just ignored that, not mentioned it at all."

Marti laughed, smoke coming out in bursts. "I could have, but then I wouldn't be rotten, would I?" She sat up straighter and added, "Time to get serious." Marti pulled her phone out, her photo app, and transferred all the car photos she'd taken.

"I searched out white cars and chop shops. You need you to search each VIN. We need to know who the current owner is, how long they've had it, and who had it before them. I'm going to contact Heather to see if she will run a stolen vehicle report for me," Marti said.

"What are you thinking?" Lori asked as the photos transferred to her computer.

"I'm thinking since she let me hold her prosthetic breast, she would be open to helping me."

"Oh my sweet–Did you really do that? Held her fake breast? How does something like that even happen?" Lori asked.

Marti smirked. "She offered. I guess she was trying–"

"No! Stop!" Lori commanded, holding up her hand. "Pretend I didn't ask that. Let's change the subject. Can we change the subject? Anything."

Marti nodded. "Swap sex stories?"

Lori closed her eyes, leaned back, and waved her hand at Marti. "Just go."

"Also, I bought a new car. Traded in the old one. A black Storm 4G. Here's the VIN. The title should be transferred by now in the system. I need proof of ownership, registration and insurance, please. Make sure it's a clean title."

"Why a new car?"

"Well, it's actually eight years old. But I wanted something a little cleaner. Something that would blend in a little more."

"Okay. Makes sense. I'll do that right now."

"You're a doll. Thanks." Marti closed the door of her office and retreated to her desk. Her cigarette dangled from her mouth, smoke boring into her eyes as she searched her phone contacts. She stubbed her cigarette out and dialed.

The phone line softly clicked. "Federal Unified Crime Taskforce. Agent Heather Blair."

"Heather. It's Marti Starova. I need your help."

"What can I do for you, Marti?" Heather asked. Marti swore she could hear the woman suddenly developing a headache and rubbing her temples.

"Have you found out who was driving the car? That hit Walter and Lori and me?"

"Ah. No, not yet. We've checked local repair shops, but came up empty. Why?" Heather asked.

"Did you check stolen car reports?"

"Of course. I'm a cop, you know." In her voice, Marti could hear the offense she'd taken.

"Yes, sorry. I meant, is there any way I can get the report from you?" Marti asked. Heather hesitated, so Marti quickly added, "Since I was a victim, too. Me and Lori both."

"No. We don't share that kind of information with victims. It leads to vigilantism," Heather said with a sigh.

"Heather, Heather. Do I seem like a vigilante to you? I'm not. I just think–"

"You weren't the target. I'm not giving you the information."

Marti gave up. She needed a better connection with Heather before asking for information of any kind. "Okay. I understand. Forget I asked. What about a drink? Not tonight. But soon? No connection to work. Just a drink?"

Marti could hear Heather tapping on her desk with her pen. She was considering it, and the thought excited Marti. After an eternity, she responded.

"Yes, okay. Like I suggested earlier. Soon."

Marti pumped her fist, excited that she might get Heather into bed. "Okay. I'll call within the week," Marti said.

"And no work."

"No work. Bye." Marti hung up and leaned back, putting her hands behind her head. She had a promise for a date, but no way to find out if a small white car had been stolen recently.

Marti dug into her drawer and took a hit of Shadow. Under the hallucinogenic haze, Marti's world warped into a surreal tableau. The edges of reality blurred, and vibrant colors painted the mundane with hallucinatory strokes. Marti's usually sharp gaze danced with disorientation as she navigated the distorted labyrinth of her perceptions.

Amidst the psychedelic swirls, a phantom feline, Bertha Tinkledorp, materialized on the fire escape. With fur that shimmered like liquid moonlight, the cat flickered in and out of existence, a whimsical guardian of the hallucinatory realm. Bertha's eyes gleamed with spectral intelligence, and her purring resonated like a hypnotic melody, weaving through Marti's altered consciousness.

The cat seemed to hold secrets in her ethereal gaze, as if the feline herself was a gatekeeper to a dimension beyond the tangible. During the trippy journey, Marti's reality and hallucination became entangled. Bertha gleamed and disappeared.

Lori walked into Marti's office, ready to report on the search for car owners. She found Marti sitting in her office chair, head back, eyes closed. Bertha sat on Marti's lap, happily purring. "So cute," Lori said as she pulled out her phone. She aimed the camera and swiftly took a photo.

Bertha had been quicker. She had taken off with such force Marti's chair moved and she grunted herself into reality. Lori looked at her photo. Marti passed out in her chair, and a furry blur exiting the image.

"Hey."

"Hey," Lori said. "You all here?"

Marti took a deep breath in and rubbed her eyes. "Yep."

Lori shook her head. "Get some cold water on your face. Come to my desk," she said. Her voice was low and somber, and it woke Marti up more than any water would. Marti watched as Lori walked out. Now what? she wondered. Marti dashed into the bathroom, slammed some water on her face, and came out scrubbing her face with a towel.

"Sit down," Lori said.

Marti frowned. She was rarely this serious. "What's up?"

"I found the car owner."

"Huh? You mean, all the car owners?"

"No. There's only one we care about. Cliff Kogoya. Sabrina's dad."

Chapter 34

Marti was silent for a moment. Leaning back, she slung her arm over the back of the chair. She studied Lori's face for signs of deception. Maybe a sick joke. Lori's eyes told her this was no joke. She did a quick mental check-in. She was ice cold. Even her fingertips were numb.

"Cliff Kogoya?" was all she could choke out. "You sure?"

Lori nodded. "Certain. Look," she said as she turned her monitor. Taking up the screen was the photo on Cliff's driver's license. The dead-eyed man stared into the middle distance. His dark hair was closely cropped, accenting his narrow face. The photographer had caught him in a frown, though it could have been permanent.

"He looks…" Marti waved her hands in front of her eyes. There was no life, no joyful youth you'd expect to see in a young man. He looked different than the last time she saw him at the restaurant. His wife Mary must give him the will to live.

"He's the mystery man. From Andreas's funeral. I'm certain it was him. He was following us," Lori said.

He tried to kill us, Marti thought.

Marti felt lightheaded. Dizziness flowed through her like her own blood. "He was the mystery man," Marti repeated. She wished her mind raced. She wished she could reason out why he tried to kill them. But her mind stayed focused on this one thing, this one man, this one traitor. She wished she could just vomit.

"Marti, I–"

Marti held up her hand to silence Lori. A wave washed over her and she didn't speak. She stood on shaky legs, made her way to the bathroom, and shut the door. She blinked in the harsh light. Had it always been that bright? Marti tried to remember Cliff's smiling face. Did he ever smile? No. He'd never smiled.

As Marti's hands clenched the edges of the sink, she could feel every molecule in her body buzzing and vibrating against each other, creating a fiery energy. It began in the pit of her stomach, churning and burning before spreading through her limbs like wildfire. The intense heat radiated up into her chest, causing her heart to pound with fury, then climbed its way to her throat, threatening to spill out in a torrent of rage-filled words. She was a volcano ready to explode, her body a vessel for all-consuming anger.

Marti had given up so much, but it just wasn't enough for Cliff. She lost herself when Kane accused her of letting Gomes escape. She lost her job, her lover, her sobriety, her self. The only thing she had done wrong was not stand up to Kane. She knew the truth, that he had set her up to take the fall, but she didn't defend herself. Marti couldn't defend herself, not then. She was young; she was trusting; she was blind. It devastated her.

But she was not that Martina Starova any more. She was innocent of wrongdoing, but she needed to be exonerated. Until the Falls City Police publicly cleared her, until they announced her innocence, she would always be guilty to Cliff. The evidence was there. They just needed to look.

Marti knew she had to make it happen. Chief Franklin refused to talk to her the last time she called. But she had an ace up her sleeve. Marti put the plug in the sink and turned on the cold water. She held her hands under the running water as it filled the sink. When it leaked into the overflow drain, she turned the water off. She drew circles in the water with her finger and plunged her face in.

The shock worked its magic, instantly cooling her boiling rage and hardening her determination. She stood in front of the mirror, her reflection distorted by the glass as she slowly dried off. But in that moment, a plan formed in her mind, crystal clear and unbreakable like a diamond.

Marti walked back into Lori's office and sat down. Lighting a cigarette, she explained her plan. Her simple plan. She would ask Keira to tell Chief Franklin about Kane's threat on her life. That would launch an internal investigation that would lead to the Kane video. Once they discovered the Kane video, it would clear Marti.

"This is the same Keira you had sex with in the office? While I hacked the police computer network?" Lori asked.

"Yes, but she didn't know you did that. There's video of me going into the office, and there will be a video of Kane going into her office. She doesn't have to say we fucked, she just has to say Kane threatened her after seeing us together. That will get everything rolling," Marti said. "I kept her safe when she was terrified of Kane. She owes me."

"What about Cliff?"

Marti stood with her arms crossed, determination etched into every line of her face. Her voice was firm and resolute as she spoke. "I'll speak to him," she declared. "I can only imagine he holds me responsible for Sabrina's death. But once the police publicly clear my name, he will have no reason to hate me. He will no longer have a motive to attempt to end my life."

Lori crossed her arms and leaned back. "Do you think he will listen?"

"Yeah," Marti said. She didn't tell Lori she was planning to take her gun, just in case he wouldn't listen. "While I'm working this, what are you working on?"

"I'm tracking two credit card transactions at The Sophet hotel that look sketchy."

"He owned the hotel. What's sketchy?"

"Exactly. He owned the hotel, so why were there two room charges? I need to follow it up," Lori said.

"Good stuff. I've got to get started. Update me later," Marti said.

Marti made a phone call to Keira, asking her to tell the Chief about Kane's threat. Keira balked at first, not wanting to raise the issue, not wanting to raise the dead.

"Keira, the truth about Kane is already coming out. His graft, his ties to gangs and drugs. His threat to you might seem minor by comparison, but if you tell Franklin, he'll have to listen. He will look into it, try to figure out why Kane cared at all about my visit. He's got other evidence on Kane, evidence that has nothing to do with you. Franklin just needs a reason to look for this one last piece of the puzzle," Marti said.

"Marti, I just don't know. What happens if they find out we had sex in the office? They could fire me. I don't want to lose my job," Keira said.

It felt to Marti like she was begging. There was no way she was going to beg Keira for anything. "You owe me," Marti said. "I saved you from Kane. I gave you a safe place to stay. You tell Franklin I was there trying to get my pension back. Period. Everything else is true. Even that's true. We just got sidetracked is all," Marti said.

Keira sighed. "Okay. I'll set up an appointment this week to see him. You really did save my life, Marti. You really did."

With that organized, Marti took a hit of Shadow. She had hours to go before she would visit Cliff and Mary. She deserved it.

After floating in the luminescent world that Shadow gave her, Lori roused Marti. "I've sent everything to your phone. Are you sure you don't want me with you?" Lori asked.

Marti shook off the cobwebs and lit a cigarette. "Yep. I got this. I'll see you tomorrow morning." Marti watched Lori leave, wondering why she was putting up such a fight against screwing that woman. She was gorgeous.

Chapter 35

Marti pulled her gun and holster out of the desk drawer and slipped it onto her belt. She thought briefly of Ha-Yoon as she grabbed her jacket and headed out.

As the sun dipped below the city's jagged skyline, Marti drove through the rain-kissed streets. The city, cloaked in the soft hues of dusk, shimmered beneath the delicate touch of raindrops, each droplet catching the fading light like liquid diamonds.

Behind the wheel, Marti exhaled a plume of smoke that curled around the confined space of the car. The rhythmic tapping of rain on the roof became a somber accompaniment to the low hum of the engine. Her eyes, a stormy gray mirroring the weather outside, were fixed on the road ahead with a determined focus.

The city's neon lights flickered to life, casting reflections on the wet asphalt. Marti's car glided through the slick streets, navigating the labyrinth of memories and intentions. The scent of rain-soaked asphalt mingled with the acrid burn of her cigarette, and creating a tapestry for her senses.

The rain intensified as Marti approached the Kogoyas's home. She parked the car, and with a final drag of her cigarette, Marti stepped out into the wet evening. She knocked.

"Oh, my goodness! Martina! Come in, come in," Mary said with a big smile. She hugged Marti. "Oh, you're wet. My gosh. Is everything okay?"

"It sure is. It was so lovely to see you at the restaurant, I had to do it again." Marti stepped in. The breath of the house was lavender and freshly baked bread. She wiped her feet and followed Mary into the living room.

"Cliff! It's Martina, come for a surprise visit."

Cliff looked up. His eyes went black and his face twisted in rage. He bolted from his chair but Marti was faster. Mary screamed when Marti pulled her gun and aimed it at Cliff. "Sit down. Both of you. Sit. Down."

"Martina! What are you doing?" Mary gasped as she sank onto the couch. Cliff stood stock still, his eyes on the gun. He groaned and rocked as if caught by a gust of wind. Finally, he fell back into his chair.

"What's going on? Someone tell me."

"Mary, shut up!" Cliff snapped. Mary swung her head to her husband sharply, her face pale.

"Cliff, don't talk to your wife like that. She deserves better. You and I need a word. Mary doesn't need to be part of this," she said.

Now Mary's terrified eyes flickered between her husband and Marti. "Cliff? What's going on?" He didn't move, not even an inch. His breathing was ragged, his body tensed. Cliff said nothing.

"You need to leave me alone, Cliff. I know it was you. You hurt more than me with your stunt," Marti said.

Cliff deflated. Mary swiveled her head between the two, her fish mouth gaping.

"Do you understand how serious this is? You hurt Lori. You really hurt that old man. I know you were at the funeral. I know you were at the bodega."

"Funeral?" Mary whispered. If she said it any louder, she thought it might be true.

Cliff groaned and sunk back, his hands flying to his face as he mumbled incoherently. His words were barely audible through the sobs that wracked his body. "Mary, I'm so sorry," he managed to choke out between gasps for air. "I just... It was eating at me. When I saw Detective Kane had died in a fire, it all just came rushing back. All the memories, all the pain... It was just too much for me to handle." The weight of his emotions seemed to physically crush him as he collapsed onto the floor, his shoulders shaking with grief.

Mary sat up, her eyes wide and wild. "Oh Cliff, what did you do?" She looked at Marti with a sudden sickness and groaned. "Did he hurt you?"

Marti shook her head. "Turns out I'm tougher than his car."

"Your car? Cliff, you said someone stole your car." Mary shook.

"No. Not stolen. Wrecked. Two other innocent people got hurt, Cliff. They'll live, but you can never come for me again. Understand?"

"If it wasn't for you–" he spat.

"I didn't do a fucking thing, Cliff. I went for coffee. I was getting coffee when Gomes attacked Kane and escaped," Marti said.

"Bullshit!" he screamed and leaped from the chair. Marti straight armed her gun, and he stopped in his tracks. There was a look in his eyes that Marti didn't understand. Was he going to suicide himself?

When he sat back down, Marti could breathe again. "It was Kane, and the police will prove it in the next month or two. Just a couple of months, and there will be an announcement."

"Someone, please. What's going on?"

Marti looked at Mary. "Are you going to tell her, Cliff, or am I? She needs to know."

Cliff's countenance betrayed the pain of an impending confession. Shame clouded his eyes, casting shadows that flickered like a guilty conscience. Lines etched deep into his forehead, forming a map of internal struggle. His hands, restless, clenched and unclenched, the subtle tremor revealing the tension within. A pallor had washed over his features. He finally spoke.

"When Detective Kane died, it brought back all that pain of losing Sabrina. And I thought, justice was finally done. He didn't deserve to be on this earth if my little girl wasn't," Cliff said with a strained voice. Tears welled in his eyes and he choked a bit. "And I thought, neither do you, Martina. You shouldn't be on this earth. You should be dead."

"Cliff!"

"Look Cliff, I'm not long for this world, but you can't help it along. You had your shot, you can't do it again.

Leave me alone. Got it?" Marti asked. Cliff nodded and lowered his head. "Did you buy a gun at that store?"

"What?" he said, shocked.

"I saw you at the gun store. That was you, wasn't it?"

Cliff nodded. "I don't have a license. They wouldn't sell to me."

Marti moved to the sofa and put her arm around Mary. She explained Cliff had been following her, looking for a chance to hurt her. He took that chance; he hurt people, and it can never happen again. She purposefully downplayed it for Mary. The woman did not need to know she was married to a man capable of such premeditated rage.

"Are you...are you going to tell the police?" Mary asked.

Marti shook her head. "No. Not if I don't have to. I don't have to, do I Cliff? No. But never again, Cliff. You got that?"

"Never," he swore. That strange, strained look came back to his eyes.

Marti knew Cliff and Mary had a lot to talk about and got up to leave, putting her gun back in its holster.

"Martina, thank you," Mary said, giving her a tight hug. "I never blamed you. Not Detective Kane either. It was that man. You found him, you caught him. You're my hero," Mary said. "My hero, in this dirty old leather jacket of yours."

"That's a new one," Cliff said as he got up to see Marti out.

Marti froze mid-step. The words hung in the air between them, innocent yet impossibly heavy. How would he know it was new? Mary hadn't noticed. No one had.

She smiled stiffly and gave Mary another hug. "I'm so sorry Mary, I really am." Her mind raced, connecting dots that had been scattered across weeks of investigation. Only one person would know her jacket was new.

She turned to Cliff, her hand moving to her holster with calm. "Mary, step back please."

"Martina, what—"

Marti pushed Mary gently aside, drawing her weapon in one fluid motion. "How did you know about my jacket, Cliff?"

Chapter 36

Marti held Cliff at gunpoint. "How do you know it's new?" Marti asked. He should not have known it was a new jacket. Not unless he knew what had happened to the old jacket.

She looked into his eyes. No. She must be wrong. Not Cliff.

Cliff held his hands out, and he wordlessly shook his head.

"Marti?" Mary sobbed, her voice breaking. "Martina, what are you doing?"

Even she wasn't sure. A pain shot through her arm just thinking of how Lori had been hurt by his car. Her body was sure.

"Did you?" Marti asked. "Mary didn't know it was new. How did you? How did you know I had a new jacket, Cliff?"

Her mind reeled. Maybe she deserved it, but Andreas? His wives and children? They didn't deserve this. Mary didn't deserve this.

"Fuck! Do you have any idea what you've done?" Marti screamed in frustration. "Cliff! Do you fucking understand who you killed?"

Mary's eyes widened in shock as she instinctively covered her mouth to stifle a scream. She squeezed her eyes shut, desperately hoping that this was just a horrible nightmare that she would soon wake up from. But the reality continued to unfold before her, refusing to fade away. The scene played out before her, each moment feeling like an eternity as she struggled to come to terms with what was happening.

"I thought it was you. I was going to confront you," he finally sobbed. "They had a mask. And it was dark. But I saw you there, outside by the hotel. I tried to follow you in. They wouldn't let me in, so I said I was a janitor, and they sent me around back. Through the kitchen. I saw all these knives just sitting there, you know? It was...automatic. Easy. It was hard to find you, but easy to take the knife. Do you know what was going on in there? Just...everywhere

I looked. I didn't want to see it, but I had to find you. And I found you. I thought I found you. I...I saw the jacket and everything went red." He lowered his eyes as they overflowed with tears. His chin quivered.

"That's why you stabbed him in the heart? You thought you were stabbing me?" Marti asked.

It was too much for Mary. She collapsed in tears, hands clenched over her ears to stop the onslaught. The suffering on her face made Marti turn away.

Marti staggered to the bathroom without a word, closing the door behind her. She gripped the sink's edge, avoiding her reflection in the mirror, and focused on breathing, just breathing. The cool porcelain anchored her to reality as her mind threatened to float away.

In the living room, Cliff remained seated, head bowed, hands clasped together as if in prayer. The silence between them stretched like a physical thing, heavy and smothering. Cliff's confession hung in the air, changing the very molecules of the space they shared.

When she returned, her face was composed but pale. Her eyes had hardened into something unreadable. She didn't sit back down, instead leaning against the doorframe, keeping distance between them.

"Tell me," she said, her voice mechanical.

"It was really horrible there. All these people and the noise…it was just…too much. I thought, 'I know that jacket.' I didn't know," Cliff said. He tried to wipe his eyes, but the tears just kept flowing. "I didn't know it was someone else."

Marti's face hardened. "You stupid man. You didn't just kill a man. You killed an important man. Shit." Marti shook her head and lowered her gun. She had to think fast.

"Mary, you need to listen. You both need to listen carefully," Marti said. She pulled Mary's hands from her head and forced her to sit up. "Listen closely."

"Cliff, the man you killed–"

"Oh my God, Cliff!"

"Andreas Katsaros. His name was Andreas Katsaros. He was a money man for a Falls City crime family. Do you understand? He was part of a large drug cartel. They want vengeance, Cliff. Do you hear me? Do you understand what that means? They will kill you. Probably Mary too."

"No, no, no!" Mary moaned as she rocked back and forth. Her tears poured down, as if her face was trying to drown the truth.

Marti waited for silence.

Chapter 37

Marti sat down and lit a cigarette. She rolled the cigarette in her fingers and scratched her head. If she told Ari, he would kill them. If she didn't tell Ari and word got out–and it would–he would kill her. Regardless of his earlier promise, he'd kill her. There was no way Marti could put her life at risk for the man who twice tried to murder her. Marti took a deep drag off her cigarette and blew the smoke out with a sigh.

Both Mary and Cliff were crying. There would be no silence. "I can give you an hour. I can give you that. You have three choices that I can see. You can pack up and run and hope you can get far enough away in an hour. But you won't get far enough away. They will find you and kill you. Or you can go to the police. I can give you the name of a federal agent who isn't on anyone's payroll. She'll arrest you and keep you safe. Just confess, but tell no one I gave you her name. She may even put Mary into witness protection. That's your second choice. That's the best choice." Marti took a deep drag.

"Is there another option?"

Marti nodded. "You can sit and wait. They'll come for you. It will probably be quick. Maybe." she said. Showing Heather's contact information to Mary, she said, "This is the agent. Take a photo. She's your best hope of living."

Shaking, Mary took a photograph of Marti's phone. "Can we have more than an hour?"

"No. If I figured it out, they may not be too far behind. You showed up at the funeral, Cliff. You fucking showed up at the funeral of the money launderer that you killed. You showed your face where you weren't invited. They will figure it out and kill you. I have to leave." Marti had learned from the Seraphina case that clients often got evidence on their own. And even when their evidence was wrong, they would act as if it was right.

"No, please!" Mary begged.

Marti shook her head. "I have to go. You have an hour. I'm sorry. I'm really sorry it went this way. One hour."

As Marti stepped out into the rain, she heard Cliff say, "Get packed." She could hear Mary sobbing.

Marti got into her car and drove away. "What a fucking waste," she cursed as she headed to the office. She slammed the steering wheel with the palms of her hands. "Fuck! Fuck! How the fuck do I explain this? To anyone?"

Marti drove to the office and parked. She watched as a dark car slowed down, then passed by. Someone had followed her. She just didn't know who. Marti walked into the building, unlocked the door, and slipped into the darkness of her office. Making her way to her inner office, she checked the time. Ten minutes left. She lit a cigarette and stared out the window.

Even in the darkness, Bertha could see her and came to the window.

Marti knew that, like Cliff, she had let her wounds fester. Her years of guilt almost destroyed her. Almost.

She opened the window to let the wet cat in and grabbed her phone. It was time. "Ari? It's Marti. I found out who killed Andreas."

"You're certain?"

"What? Yes, I am one hundred percent certain. He confessed to me. Just now. I've been in my office for maybe ten minutes. I'll send you the information in a minute." Marti turned on the computer, tapped a few keys, and sent Ari a copy of Cliff's driver's license.

She wasn't sure how to feel. Cliff was a grieving father who lost his child in a horrible murder. Marti had nothing to do with Sabrina's death. Neither did Lori, nor Walter fucking Lewis. But he became a murderer, killing an innocent man. Andreas was a scoundrel, sure, but he had nothing to do with Sabrina's death and did not deserve to die. Cliff had fucked over three families, including his own, with his actions. Cliff had to face the consequences of his actions. Marti had always dealt with the fallout from her decisions. At least the big ones.

"He killed your man by mistake. Thought it was me," Marti told Ari.

"How the fuck could anyone think Andreas was you?" Ari snapped.

Marti sighed and gave Bertha a push to get the cat off her desk. "Andreas was wearing my leather jacket. This guy knew the jacket. When he saw it, he stabbed. Nothing more to it than that, really."

"Why did he want you dead?"

"Because he's an asshole."

"You're usually the asshole."

"Yeah, but I didn't kill anyone. Ergo, not the asshole. Not this time," Marti said with a sigh. "Ari, it's complex. And I don't know if it really matters. I'm telling you because you're my client, and you hired me to find out who killed Andreas. I did. That's the end. I don't owe you an explanation, just the evidence. And remember your promise."

"You're right Starova, you're right. You don't owe me an explanation. You know what's going to happen. And I know this guy must be guilty, or you wouldn't have told me," Ari said. "I'll pay the invoice. Good doing business with you."

Marti took off her jacket and laid down on the couch. Bertha jumped up with a peep and head-butted Marti. She had no food, no litter box. But here Bertha was anyway.

"You're just here for the warmth, aren't you?" she asked as she gave Bertha a scratch. It took hours of restless thought, but Marti finally fell asleep. Bertha laid on her chest.

Chapter 38

"Wake up. Marti, wake up." Lori shook her shoulder to disturb her slumber. It was morning, and the sun was almost breaking through the clouds. Marti had fallen into a restless sleep after turning Cliff over to Ari. Whatever was to happen, already happened. Bertha was gone. Only Lori was there. It is just me and her, like always.

"Heather Blair is here," Lori said. "Do you have some time to see her?"

Make that me, her and Heather. Marti's heart jumped. "Yeah, yeah, let her in." Does that mean Cliff made it to Heather? Or did Heather pick up his homicide? There was only one way to find out.

"Fix yourself first, then come out," Lori said as she ran her fingers through Marti's hair.

Lori walked out and Marti headed to the bathroom to fix herself. Heather was hot, and Marti wanted to look fuckable.

"Hey," Marti said, stepping into Lori's office with a smile.

Heather had a huge smile on her face. "Your client, Elizabeth Preston, is going to be released," she said proudly. She was sitting perched in the chair, her back straight and her head up.

Relief flooded over Marti, and she sat down, throwing Lori a look. "She was never my client. Her daughter was. Why are you releasing her?"

Heather sat even taller and said, "A man named Cliff Kogoya called me last night, confessed to killing Andreas. He had details no one else had. Things only the killer would know. We picked him up at his home."

Lori leaned back in her chair, slack-jawed and wide eyed. Did you? she mouthed.

Marti winked and lit a cigarette. Her plan worked. "Does Ria know about her mom?"

"Yes."

"And what did this Cliff guy say to you?" Marti asked.

"He said he'd taken some drugs–"

"See Lori, I told you drugs are bad," Marti smirked. Heather gave her a look.

"He'd taken some drugs, and somehow ended up in the club. He isn't sure how he got there. And he said he saw monsters. He attacked a monster that he thought was attacking a woman. That's what he's saying, anyway. The story is a little shaky if you ask me. But he has details, very clear details on the stabbing," Heather said. "He said he saw my name in the media about the case and needed to confess. That's all I can tell you right now. The rest you'll have to read in the press release. It will be out later today."

"Thanks, I appreciate you letting us know," Marti said, standing as Heather also stood up. She extended her hand. "I hope it goes smoothly for you."

Heather shook her hand. "I'm confident."

Marti wanted to kiss her lips, hold her hips. She had to settle for a smile. "What about that drink?"

Heather shook her head. "You still have a..." She gave a sideways glance at Lori. "An issue to resolve. Which I hope resolves soon. I'd like that drink." Marti knew Heather was referring to her arrest, acting as if Lori didn't know every part of her life.

Heather walked out, and Lori closed the door behind her. Leaning with her back against the door, Lori raised her eyebrow at Marti. "How the hell?"

"He said something about my new jacket. The only reason he would know it was new was if he knew what happened to the old one," Marti said.

Lori pushed herself off the door. "But it's an obviously new jacket."

"Only because you were familiar with the old one," Marti said. "I saw them once a year. Mary thought it was the old jacket. She even said so. Cliff corrected her because he knew."

"And you told him to contact Heather?"

"Yeah," Marti said, finishing her cigarette. "But I told Ari, too. He'd have found out as soon as they announced an arrest, so I had to get ahead of that. But Cliff made it to the Feds, and that's his best chance."

Lori lowered her eyes, then raised them to meet Marti's. "Martina Starova, you are something else." She stepped forward, eyes lowered, looking at Marti's lips.

The door opened abruptly and bumped into her. Heather popped her head in. "Oops, sorry, I didn't know you were right there. Am I interrupting?" She stepped in.

"No, what is it?" Marti asked, wiping her mouth. Lori sat down.

"I think I would like that drink. As a celebration. It's early, so maybe coffee?" Heather asked brightly.

"Fucking coffee. Yeah, sure. Coffee sounds great," Marti said. She might get laid this morning, after all. "You good?" she said to Lori, looking deeply into her eyes.

"Better than you think," Lori replied with a wink.

Marti and Heather headed out, walking down the stairs. "I parked my car out front. A nice black Storm 4G. New. To me, anyway. We'll take my car." They got to the ground floor and Marti pushed the door open.

She stepped into the gun of Ari Stirling.

"What the fuck, Ari?" She stopped in her tracks, Heather immediately behind her.

"What's—" That was all Heather could say. She looked around. A man with a gun just feet away, and another half-dozen men with automatic weapons. All pointed at them.

"Ari, put your dick away and talk to me."

"My dick? How about this little side piece of yours? I get it now. I get why you told Cliff to contact her. You're fucking her, and you want a bonus from her. But he was my prize, Starova. Mine. He belonged to me." Ari was furious that he'd lost out on his chance to wreak vengeance.

"No, Ari, you have that wrong. Not a side piece. She's arresting me again," Marti said. She hoped to at least save Heather's life if he was going to start shooting. "I didn't tell anyone to contact her."

Ari shook his head. "Bullshit."

"Ari, I didn't. But even if I did, it doesn't matter. You...have a long reach." She gave him a meaningful look. Marti didn't want to say too much in front of Heather. She only wanted to remind him that Cliff would never be out of his reach.

Ari drew in a deep breath and lowered his gun. "Fuck. You're right. Fuck, sorry. I just have to wait a day or two."

"A day or two." Marti knew he'd have Cliff killed while he was in custody. She'd hoped he would show a little humanity. But he had none.

To her right, Marti heard a noise and turned.

Epilogue

Lori was working diligently at her desk when the roar of gunfire shattered the tranquility of her office. Ten seconds and at least a thousand shots, she was sure. It was so close she could feel the vibrations in her bones. Without hesitation, Lori dropped to the floor and scrambled under her desk, heart pounding. She had barely hit the floor by the time it all stopped.

"What the hell?" Lori bolted out of her seat and stormed into Marti's office so she could look out the window. She pushed open the door so hard it slammed against the wall. Her eyes scanned the dark city streets below, searching for the danger. Rain pelted against the window, creating puddles that seemed to swirl and churn with sinister intent. Neon lights flickered in the distance, casting an eerie glow over the streets below. Puddles of rain. Flashes of reflected neon. A glowing light. Nothing more.

Marti and Heather had left just minutes previously. Nervously, Lori called Marti to make sure she was alright. Looking down on the ground, she still saw nothing but neon and light. No answer. She hung up and tentatively opened the window to get a clearer view.

Looking past the fire escape, she called Marti again. That light. It just lit up again. No answer. Lori hung up. The light went out.

A ferocious chill surged through Lori's body, causing her to shiver uncontrollably. She dialed one more time; the light came on. She hung up; it went out.

"NO! NO!" That was a phone, and it belonged to Marti. Without hesitation, Lori leaped out of the window and raced down the fire escape. Maniacally pressing 911, she screamed for an ambulance, for police, for anyone who could help. Her voice trembled as she blurted out the address before descending the last flight. It was a nightmare. It was a nightmare come to life. Men lay scattered on the ground, some already dead and others clinging onto their last breaths. Ari. Heather. And there, lying motionless near them, was Marti.

The sound of Lori's piercing screams tore through the air as she ran towards Marti's body, stumbling over her own feet in desperation.

"No, no, no!" she wailed, collapsing onto her knees and reaching out to touch Marti's cold, pale face. Tears streamed down her cheeks as she cradled Marti's head in her lap, horrified by the sight of her damaged body. The metallic scent of blood filled her nostrils as she watched it mix with the rain, a rivulet of death flowing into the drain. Lori's heart shattered into a million pieces. This couldn't be real. It couldn't be happening. It can't happen. But it did.

Marti's blood looked almost radiant in the neon-lit rain. Almost.

Continue the Falls City Series

What happens next? Find out in ***The Familiar Dark*** - March 11, 2026

In Book 5 of the Marti Starova Thriller series, PI Marti Starova starts looking for missing young men. Her actions set off a chain of events that will see her lose what she loves most in the name of justice.

Ready to keep reading? Pre-order now!